I0538543

SOLSTICE

MILTON WORKSHOP ANTHOLOGY SERIES
WINTER 2017

DEVIL'S PARTY PRESS

Solstice.
Milton Workshop Anthology Series: Winter 2017
Copyright © 2017 by Devil's Party Press.
Designed and edited by David Yurkovich.
All stories contained within this anthology are copyright the
respective authors. All rights reserved. Any similarities between
actual persons, places, or events are entirely coincidental.

ISBN: 978-0-9722646-9-3

ACKNOWLEDGMENTS

WINTERS ATTIC. Copyright © 2017 D. Beals. Reprinted with permission of the author.

ON GEORGIAN BAY. Copyright © 2017 William F. Crandell. Reprinted with permission of the author.

COOPERSMITH'S. Copyright © 2017 David W. Dutton. Reprinted with permission of the author.

ELIZA'S CHRISTMAS. Copyright © 2017 David W. Dutton. Reprinted with permission of the author.

THE SNOW MONKEY. Copyright © 2017 T.J. Lewes. Reprinted with permission of the author.

PAW PRINTS IN THE SNOW. Copyright © 2017 Bayne Northern. Reprinted with permission of the author.

BLACKBERRY WINTER. Copyright © 2017 Dianne Pearce. Reprinted with permission of the author.

DIGGIN' OUT THE DOG. DRIVING HOME AFTER THE HOLIDAYS. AFTER YOU LEAVE. Copyright © 2017 Dianne Pearce. Reprinted with permission of the author.

WINTER EYES. Copyright © 2017 Mark Alan Polo. Reprinted with permission of the author.

RAIN WITH PIANO. Copyright © 2017 Judith Speizer Crandell. Reprinted with permission of the author.

THE CHRISTMAS LETTER I NEVER SENT. Copyright © 2017 Carrie Sz Keane. Reprinted with permission of the author.

A COUGH AT THE COLLEGE OF THE PACIFIC. Copyright © 2017 David Yurkovich. Reprinted with permission of the author.

PHOTO CREDIT

HISTORIC MILTON DELAWARE: FEDERAL STREET LOOKING TOWARD BROADKILL (circa early 1900s). Reproduced with kind permission of The Milton Historic Society, Milton, DE.

**Also Available in the
Milton Workshop Anthology Series**

HALLOWEEN PARTY 2017
(ISBN 097226468X)

CONTENTS

The Winter Solstice is the time of ending and beginning,
a powerful time–a time to contemplate your immortality.
A time to forgive, to be forgiven, and to make a fresh start.
A time to awaken.

Frederick Lenz

People don't notice whether it's winter or summer
when they're happy.

Anton Chekov

SOLSTICE

PREFACE

THE WINTER SOLSTICE IS SPECIAL to most of us. It embodies the holidays and brings forth cherished memories of times past. With each new season, we're reminded of what has come before; though perhaps no season invokes this spirit more so than winter. It is a time during which new memories are made and old ones are revisited year after year.

Within this anthology, you'll find original material from each member of The Milton Workshop. Included is wonderful poetry, warm and heartfelt prose, and a unique missive in the form of a Christmas letter. I'll refrain from spoiling the tales and will instead let you discover them for yourself.

The cover photo for this volume was graciously provided by the Milton Historical Society. It embodies all that I remember as a child growing up in Milton. Back in the day, we enjoyed snow falls with regularity, and there are many tales associated with those times.

One of my favorite memories involves sledding. In my youth, the Lawson family lived in the big, brick Queen Anne Victorian now occupied by Bob Blayney and Libby Zando. In those days, nothing stood between the house and the river but a massive, sloping yard, the perfect setting for a downhill flight aboard a Flexible Flyer. As soon as the first major snowfall arrived, it seemed as if the entire town converged in the Lawson's back yard.

There simply was no better place to sled, no better locale for winter merriment and childhood shenanigans. Norman Lawson illuminated the slope with bright white spotlights mounted on the eaves of his house, enabling us to frolic long into the evening hours. Meanwhile, Marie Lawson dispensed mugs of warm cocoa to kids with red cheeks and near-frozen fingers. Hours passed as young and old alike took to the hill, a sled in hand. In retrospect, those winter days seem like a Christmas-time lithograph printed by Currier and Ives.

I still recall the day of the accident. My parents had commandeered my sled for a trip down the slippery hill. Mom was seated in front between my Dad's outstretched legs. I'd cheered as they soared down the steep slope but soon gasped as, seconds later, they hit a hillock, and the sled went airborne. They'd escaped unharmed, but my sled did not, having been splintered in two beneath their combined weight. Still, the sight had been worth the sacrifice, and I even got a new sled in the bargain.

Now it's time for you to jump on that sled and follow us to the bottom of the hill. I promise you, it'll be well worth the trip.

DAVID W. DUTTON
Milton, Delaware

WINTER EYES

Mark Alan Polo

"SEE, THAT'S YOU AND THAT'S LES," Sam said to Renee as he held the scrapbook and turned the pages. Renee had trouble focusing, but her own photo held her interest.

"That's me?" she asked. It was encouraging that she recognized her own image.

"Yes . . . and Les." Les and Renee had been married for sixty years. The photo was from the 1940s when they were first dating. They summered in Fenwick Island that year. The photo depicted them on the beach beneath a striped cabana awning. They were a striking couple. She was a violet-eyed beauty with light brown flowing hair, and statuesque in height. Renee had the bearing and body language of a more affluent person, someone who'd grown up in wealth instead of dancing around it from her actual birthplace, an apartment in Brooklyn. Les, a former marine had been a privileged upbringing of wealth, boarding schools, and nannies. He graduated from a South Carolina military school. Les and Renee met on Fenwick Island that year; and, under that striped awning he fell in love with those violet eyes. She returned the affection of the well-muscled man, six-foot three in height with wavy blonde locks. From that moment, that photo, they were inseparable. He would tell of their first meeting to all who'd listen.

Whenever Sam sat with Renee they were hopeful that she would remember, hoped that somewhere locked in the jumbled signals coursing around in her brain that this photo would hit a spark.

Renee paused for a moment and touched Les' image on the photo. She looked deep in thought and a slight smile crossed her lips. She looked at Sam and said, "It's a lovely photo. That's him in the other room?"

"Yes. Your husband Les is in the other room." Sam felt relieved that there was progress in her memory of Les.

"Well," She said, "He's a very nice man . . . a gentleman. But, I don't know who he is."

"Are you sure? Look, again," Sam asked, sadly knowing the outcome.

Renee looked over her shoulder and said, "He's in the next room, isn't he? He's very handsome, too."

Les was nearing eighty-five but held on to the proud demeanor of a life well designed and executed with a face that aged into kindness.

Renee tried to offer more, "Well," I know he lives here and he certainly is kind. I don't know him though. But," she said in a confidential whisper, "I do know that he's very rich."

She couldn't recognize her spouse but she still understood her environment and its trappings.

Renee sat in the living room of their palatial apartment in the heart of Beverly Hills and remembered nothing of buying the home, furnishing it with Sam's help, and moving into it with Les some three years before. Her deterioration was rapid, and everyone felt the onslaught.

It had been more than two years ago since Renee announced her devastating conclusions at a dinner party in their apartment on a balmy Saturday evening. She'd stood up in front of her seat and held onto the table, "I just want everyone to know that I believe I have Alzheimer's."

"Oh for God's sakes, Renee! You are so dramatic!" Ivan, a retired film executive had reprimanded, "We all have moments of forgetfulness."

"No, Ivan. This is more than a forgetful moment or two. And I am not going to ignore it anymore. I want my friends to know."

"We have been to the doctors," Les explained. "All signs point to this." He'd sat slumped in his chair staring at the table. He was very used to Renee going full-steam ahead when it came to her passions and had learned years ago not to get in front of the fast-moving train.

The room had fallen silent while everyone faced their mortality.

"I don't want to put a pallor on the evening, but I wanted all of you together. I've said it, now let's move on."

The evening hadn't been quite the same after that. At the end of the night, the couples had all hugged at the door knowing that changes were happening and that no matter how insulated they might be from other things, this was something beyond their control.

Sam hugged Renee's sister–in-law, Louise. "Don't let her get lost," she'd whispered in his ear.

Sam didn't know how to prevent that eventuality. He thought that the announcement had been Louise's way of letting it all go, and he was right. Soon after that fateful evening, Louise and her husband, unwilling to bear witness to Renee's inevitable decline, began to separate from friends and family and quickly listed their house on the market. They were gone within three months. These were among the unintended consequences of truth. Les never allowed his hurt to show, but following Louise's departure his lean and tall stature diminished. With Louise out of the picture, Les realized that he had to shoulder this alone.

Whenever Renee descended into her dark vacant periods, Les referred to it as her "winter eyes." Renee's transition into winter eyes was fast and frequent. Les always knew when she was absent from the conversation, her intense violet eyes visibly faded. "It was as if winter's cold blast blew into her eyes," he said.

When he saw it, as the months went on, he knew enough to stop and let patience and time wash over him.

Several months passed before they saw Sam again. People of wealth always traveled with their essentials: appropriate attire, passport, their portfolio and their Interior Designer. Sam being among the best, it was easy to incorporate him into their family and social circle. So, when summoned, he ran, always staying with them making sure that his plane ticket was open ended. He was like a son to them. Their time together linked them on so many levels that distance had little effect on their relationship. Over the years they explored and laughed and enjoyed unique and special moments far and above their initial designer-client business relationship.

Renee still remembered Sam, but it was unclear as to whether or not she remembered their thirty-five–year involvement in designing all of their residences throughout the years. Sam sometimes spoke about the fun they had in one house or another, the picnics at their farm house, or fireworks viewed from a window overlooking the East River, from their first beach house on Fenwick Island, onto East Hampton, and finally Beverly Hills where life rapidly unraveled. Each time he did, there was less and less response from Renee.

It was Sam's routine now. Like clockwork, he would arrive at their apartment and sit in the living room with Renee and they would look through the photo album together. He closed the album just as Les entered the living room.

"Any luck?" He asked, knowing the answer.

"No," Sam said, "it seems to have gotten worse."

Renee looked up and poked at Sam. "See? Rich." She thought she'd whispered. Renee's response had seem to deteriorate since the last time Sam visited with her. They relived the exact moment over and over with less and less response.

Les' forehead produced an immediate furrow. "That's it. We're moving."

"Moving?" Sam asked.

"Yes, we're going back to Fenwick Island."

"Fenwick Island?" Sam said, incredulously.

"Yup, we're going back."

"But Les, it's January. It's warm and sunny here on Wilshire, but remember it's cold and dank on the East Coast. You're not used to that anymore."

"We'll get used to it. There's no reason for us to be here any-more. I've had my fill of the distance, the palm trees, and the traffic of the 405. I am bone tired and this is the last move that I have left in me. I want to go back. We need to go back. Maybe starting from the beginning. I can stall the darkness, the winter."

"But . . . winter in the East, Les . . ."

"Sam," Les abruptly interrupted, "It's not the winter in the East that worries me. It's the winter I have in my own home, in my Renee." He looked at her and stroked her hair. She looked up at him and smiled politely.

"Where are we going?" Renee asked. She had been distracted by the cover of the antique photo album and was fingering its edges and inlays.

"We're going back to Fenwick, Renee." Les said, as his eyes softened looking at her.

"I remember Fenwick Island. I remember my house there with my family. I liked it there. You know, that's where I met my husband," she said with winter eyes.

"Yes, kiddo, I remember. We need to do this right away."

He left Renee and Sam in the room and began his mission. Les phoned packers, movers, and his real-estate agent. He also phoned his travel agent, who was more accustomed to booking trips abroad and cruises.

"We are leaving here by the end of the week," Les said to the agent. "Get me tickets to the airport in Philly and a car service to Fenwick Island, Delaware. Yes, that's right, Fenwick. I'll give you the address as soon as I know it. Probably call you this afternoon, late."

Within two days the apartment was packed up with the possessions of sixty years being boxed and wrapped, tossed, or given away. This was going to be a lean move consisting of a combination of things they needed and things Renee loved and remembered. By the end of the second day of planning, there were three first-class tickets going east.

Sam canceled his plans for the next couple of weeks, as any mission that Les decided to begin, he was immediately on board. Sam's connection to Les and Renee went well beyond designer and client. They'd saved his life years ago. They'd done so by not forgetting their connection, one that transcended furniture and fringe. Divorce is hard, and when Sam went through his, there were no papers, no legalities. A gay couple had no laws entering into a relationship and even fewer when the exit needed to happen. There was just proving what you owned, why, and how much. After twelve years of growing the roots of the tree, it took another three for Sam to extricate from the debris of unaddressed angers and upsets. Three years to fight a fight with no rules. Through it all, Renee and Les kept their relationship with Sam on an even keel, involving him socially with dinners and coming over to his temporary and paltry apartment, pretending it was wonderful. They invited him out to events in the city and had projects for him into which to sink his design teeth. They made it life as usual for Sam, always talking about the future and never the present.

Les rented a beachside house in the south end of Fenwick Island. He knew it was right as soon as he'd seen the photos. It was near the same spot, just two houses away, where sixty years earlier his adventure with Renee had begun. It's where he'd first seen violet eyes, violet eyes that burned intensely with intelligence and wit and fun. He remembered this house as that of his childhood friend. Although six decades created accidental and deliberate differences, it was still in its core the house of his childhood. They'd lived there during the summer that year, so long ago, at the edge of the sea. The house was called "Road's End." He took it for the winter, what was left, and made sure that he could extend for a longer time, if necessary.

Twenty boxes of personal items were delivered to their new beach house along with their clothing. The rest went into storage. Sam arranged the familiar possessions on all of the furniture that filled the rental home. Everything Renee remembered, touched, and held throughout the last two months was placed in her path. The mission was completed in less than ten days.

"I've always loved this place," Renee said as she walked through the rooms unescorted. "I'm glad we're back." She held onto walls and walked in looser circles than in Beverly Hills. She was less agitated and more relaxed in this environment. Whether it was the salt air or the sound of the waves continually crashing on the shoreline, something softened Renee's tense demeanor.

Les, his work finally finished, allowed himself to relax. The move took a lot out of him and at eighty-five this kind of disruption was not for the weak willed. Sam left Les and Renee to their own devices as he bade his friends farewell.

"If there's anything you need, anything, just let me know," he said.

He kissed Renee on the cheek and Les on the forehead as he sat next to Renee in total exhaustion. Les stood up and walked Sam to the door. Renee followed in a quick shuffle.

He closed the door of the car, knowing that there was a distinct possibility he was closing the door on life as he knew it. This would be the last time that he would see Renee. She stood on the front porch facing the road and waved him a goodbye, alternating with the kisses that she would exaggerate from the beginning. She hadn't done that in a long time. Something changed. Sam smiled, leaned back, and sighed the sigh of loss and closure.

Les held Renee by the shoulders. "Want to sit on the beach?" he suggested.

"I would love that, but it's cold out." She did not use his name, but Les was surprised that Renee was more comfortable with the suggestion that he'd made.

"I know, but we should celebrate our being back here, shouldn't we?" Les looked at the details of her face, wanting to remember this moment somehow.

He quickly gathered up the blankets before the moment was gone. Renee looked in the mirror and adjusted the hat she'd placed on her head. She looked in the mirror and used her pinky finger to smooth the lipstick that Les helped her to apply earlier that morning.

"It takes longer and longer to look worse and worse," she said as she inspected further.

There was no telling what she saw in that reflection. Her violet eyes were still there, although not as big as they once were and certainly not as rich in color. Her thin trumpet nose was evident but its landscape was rougher. She smiled through wrinkles that had grown from year to year. Beneath it all remained the beauty that formed the original, only now with more layers that wisdom and loss bestows.

They left for the sand right outside their door and sat on a blanket that Les spread. Renee had no concept of time or distance. It could have been five minutes or one hour that they'd walked. Time didn't matter to either of them at that moment, though for different reasons.

Les gently adjusted the coat on Renee's shoulders as she was always colder than the temperature planned. He wrapped a scarf around her neck slid gloves over her hands. Les sat down, enveloping himself and Renee in a big and heavy wool blanket to stave off the nor'east wind.

"How you doing, kiddo?" Les looked at her violet eyes as he

asked.

She looked at him then gazed at the ocean before leaning into his shoulder as his arm reached around and covered the protection of the blanket.

"When were we here last, Les?" she asked. "I can't remember."

He stuttered for a minute. It was the first time in months that she had spoken his name. "It has been years, kiddo."

Les looked at Renee's hair as she leaned in. He petted her head with long strokes of his hand. "It's nice to have you back for a bit, kiddo."

A tears welled up in his eyes but he was too much of a marine to let them fall.

"Yes, Les, where have you been? Don't ever leave me alone this long again," she reprimanded. Her violet eyes stared back at him with more intensity than they'd had in months. The winter in her eyes was gone.

"I'll never leave you again, I promise," he said.

Time drifted gently from history and back to the present like the tide. Les was right. They needed to be there at this point in time. He watched the waves filter over the sand and push a light line of foam over the granular grooves.

They sat there, nestled against the cold wind, huddled together against the onslaught of the future. And this was what they would do each day through the cold of winter and the warming turn of spring, for as long as time would allow.

THE SNOW MONKEY

T.J. Lewes

Blind retribution,
Consequences, dominoes,
Crashing to the ground.

RYUU WAS NOT POPULAR, affluent, or beloved. He did not have proud parents who walked him to school, a clean and pressed uniform, or a bento box full of fresh fruit, tempura, rice, and edamame. He did not play Keidoro tag with the other children during recess, or join in the games of Oni Gokko after classes. He did not go home at night to a loving family, a filling dinner, or a comfortable bed.

The orphanage, the place Ryuu had called home for his entire life, was a run-down, faded structure on the outskirts of Yamanouchi, Japan. It was understaffed and underfunded, making the employees overworked and overwhelmed. In their efforts to stay on top of the workload, the staff dropped the children to the bottom of the priority list. No hugs, kisses, playtime, cuddles, books, games, songs, toys, laughter, joy, light, warmth, or hope. The children survived, but they did not thrive.

In the early years, Ryuu tried to combat the overwhelming emptiness in his life by befriending his fellow orphans. However, one by one, as his companions were adopted, Ryuu was left feeling lonelier than before. By age seven, he no longer tried to make friends with the new kids; it hurt too much to lose them. He was quiet and obedient, but guarded and withdrawn. Hopeful families always overlooked him.

At school, Ryuu tried to be a standout student, but his humble existence was barely acknowledged by the teachers and staff. Most classmates ignored him completely, except for the ones who made fun of him. They paid him far too much attention.

"Look at wrinkled Ryuu. His shirt is as creased as a Shar-pei!"

"There are more holes in his shoes than fish in the ocean!"

"Shoes? They look more like canoes!"

"His pants are so short, he looks like he's ready to go wading!"

Everything they said was true. He outgrew his pants the year before, but longer ones were not available. His old shoes had gotten so tight that his toenails fell out, and the blisters on his heels bled onto the orphanage floor. The maintenance man cleaning the mess had taken pity on Ryuu, and brought an old pair of his own shoes to the boy. They were too large, and resembled Swiss cheese, but Ryuu gladly accepted them.

Each night, Ryuu slept on the floor, upon a thin tatami mat, with a threadbare blanket from his infancy that only covered him when he curled into a ball. He used his school uniform as a pillow. It made his clothes wrinkle, but at least he could sleep a little. Without so much as a fusuma panel to separate him from the others, he was awoken often.

The summers were hot, the spring and fall were bearable, but in the long, harsh winter, the boy suffered. Snow covered the ground for four months straight, but the temperature dropped below freezing much earlier. The cold seeped up through the floorboards, and frigid drafts blew under the doors for half the year. Ryuu always wore his gym outfit over top his pajamas, covered by his coat and blanket, but he still shivered himself to sleep every night and always woke up numb and stiff the next morning. The meager breakfast of Nattō, consisting of rice and fermented soy beans, did little to warm him.

The walk to school was long and difficult, especially in the snow and ice. Ryuu wore two pairs of socks every day, but his feet were always wet and frozen when he arrived. By the time his feet had dried and thawed, class was over, and he had to make the journey again. Every evening he hung his socks to dry and slept barefoot.

One night in early February, a fierce storm covered the town in nearly three feet of snow. It took Ryuu almost two hours to clamber through the drifts to school. He arrived late, and was castigated by the teacher in front of the entire class. As punishment, he was forced to stand in the corner the rest of the day, without lunch or bathroom breaks, balancing a book on his head. His constant shivering made the book fall often. Every time the book hit the floor, the teacher hit him.

Ryuu knew that the school would contact the orphanage about his bad behavior. No doubt he would be punished harshly that night. His belly growled, his frozen and wet feet hurt, and his body ached from trying to stand still, but he did not cry in front of the other students.

After school, several of his classmates waited for him outside. As soon as Ryuu exited the building, they pummeled him with snow balls, taunting him and calling him names. One child, the headmaster's son Takeshi, threw a chunk of ice. It hit Ryuu in the face, gashing his cheek.

Ryuu retrieved the chunk of ice from the ground and threw it as hard as he could. It smashed Takeshi on the forehead and the boy crumbled to the ground unconscious. Within moments, several concerned students, school staff, and town folk had huddled around the fallen child. It didn't take long for the fingers to point at Ryuu.

Without a thought, he turned and fled, away from the school, the orphanage, and the town. The thick snow slowed him, and the fierce wind pounded his small frame, but Ryuu ran for hours until his weary legs could go no farther. Only then did he notice his surroundings. He had wandered deep into the Jigokudani Park, otherwise known as Hell's Valley. Twilight had already descended and soon the forest would be black and impenetrable.

The thought of spending the night alone in the wilderness frightened him, but the idea of returning to the town scared him even more. He looked around frantically for refuge from the relentless wind, but the dying light made it difficult to see farther than a few feet ahead of him. He stumbled forward, toward an overturned tree, his exhausted legs trembling from exertion and cold. Before he reached it the ground below gave way.

Ryuu rode the wave of snow to the bottom of a ravine. The steep walls blocked the wind, and a thermal spring steamed in front of him. He knew that some of the springs were too hot to touch and would burn the skin off his body. He stared at the water, trying to see if there were dangerous boiling bubbles in the darkness. He couldn't tell for sure.

He touched the water hesitantly with his left hand for a few seconds. His fingers were too cold to determine the temperature, but his skin didn't blister. After a moment of thought, Ryuu fumbled off his shoes and socks, and thrust his frozen feet into the heated spring.

After 20 seconds, he evaluated his feet carefully. The skin was cracked, and his toenails had not grown back yet, but his feet didn't appear to be burnt by the water. In fact, they were beginning to thaw. Ryuu stripped naked and immersed his whole body.

Within minutes, his body felt thawed; for the first time since summer, he felt warm. It was glorious. Ryuu's fatigue, coupled by the comfort of the spring, pulled him toward sleep. It took every ounce of his determination and energy to pull himself out of the blissful heat and into the freezing air, but he knew that he would surely die if he stayed in the water.

He dressed quickly, and curled himself on the edge of the spring where no snow coated the ground. The surrounding air was warm, and the darkness complete. Instead of the cries of other children, he heard only the silence of Hell's Valley in winter. Despite his hunger and his angst, Ryuu soon fell into a deep sleep.

The sound of crunching ice and snow jolted the small boy awake. He opened his eyes, but did not move. Ryuu's body was paralyzed with fear. He had heard many tales about the demons and Oni that inhabited the mountains. His breathing quickened as he strained his eyes to see through the steam in the early morning sun.

The specter arrived at the water's edge across from him, before Ryuu even saw it approach. It had a red face, brown eyes, and black fingers. The brown-grey fur, tipped with ice, stuck up wildly in all directions. For a moment, Ryuu's heart stopped. Then, he realized the creature stood less than two feet tall and probably weighed a mere twenty pounds.

Slowly, Ryuu sat up to get a better look at the snow monkey. He had never seen one before, but he learned about the saru in school. These macaques lived in the mountain range surrounding his town, and often bathed in the hot springs during winter. The snow monkey sat down and returned the gaze quizzically across steaming water. The boy and the macaque were less than ten feet apart.

Ryuu sat as still as he could, but he had never been so excited in his life. The animal across from him seemed more like a spirit messenger than a corporeal creature. Suddenly, Ryuu wondered if he was dreaming. He pinched his leg hard and cried out from the pain. The snow monkey leapt to its feet, startled by the sound. It ran a few yards to a nearby tree and scrambled up the icy branches. Halfway to the top, it slipped and crashed to the ground below, covered in a mound of snow and ice.

Ryuu was horrified. He ran to the tree and began digging away the heavy snow with his hands. The ice cut his fingers, but he did not stop until he found the snow monkey, buried a foot down. Carefully, he cleared the snow away from the animal. He could tell immediately that the macaque's front leg was broken. It laid angled in the opposite direction. The animal did not move, but its eyes followed Ryuu's every action.

Ryuu didn't know what to do. The poor animal in front of him would surely die without help, but he didn't even know how to take care of himself. He knew the animal was cold, needed medical aid, and would probably be hungry. His own belly growled viciously, reminding him that he hadn't eaten since breakfast the day before.

The snow monkey began to tremble. Ryuu didn't know if it was from cold, fear, or pain, but it made his heart break. Tentatively, he reached out his hand and stroked the macaque's back. He didn't know if it made the little creature feel better, but the animal stopped shaking. Within minutes, Ryuu devised a plan.

Carefully, he carried the little saru to the hot spring, where the warm water would help it thaw. He tried not to jostle its broken arm, but it still whimpered when he set it on the bank. He stepped back to give the snow monkey space. After a moment, it slid into the water, resting its broken arm on the bank.

Ryuu removed one pair of socks and filled them with snow. When he was sure the animal was warm and calm, he placed the stuffed, frozen socks on either side of the break to reduce the swelling. He knew the macaque would need a splint, but he was not sure what he could tie it with. His stomach growled again.

The boy looked once more at the snow monkey, before trekking out of the ravine in search of food, splints, and a tie. Every hundred yards, Ryuu made a little pyramid of sticks to help him find his way back to the hot spring. The wind abated early in the morning, but it had blown snow over his tracks from the night before. He had no idea how to get to the village.

It took Ryuu several hours to forage enough food for himself and for his companion. The deep snow made walking difficult, and food was sparse. His pockets were full of Goma seeds, leaves, and stems from the Fukinoto plant, and Warabi fern roots. He carried the best in his hands: several tangerines completely encrusted in ice. He followed his stick pyramids back to the hot spring, but did not see the snow monkey when he arrived.

Ryuu looked around desperately, but only found his socks by the water's edge. After a long day roaming the winter mountains, he was too cold and weary to search for the animal. Instead, he stripped his clothes and gratefully submerged himself into the steaming water. When he surfaced, the macaque stood on the shore in front of him. They locked eyes.

Moving very slowly, Ryuu reached one arm out to retrieve some food from his coat pocket. He laid the roots in front of the snow monkey, then Ryuu retreated into the spring, chewing on a handful of Fukinoto leaves. He took two ice-covered tangerines with him, holding them underwater. The macaque sniffed the greens carefully, then sat down at the water's edge to eat, eyes still glued to Ryuu.

The snow monkey's left arm hung limply at its side, still twisted oddly. Ryuu couldn't tell for sure, but the limb didn't seem very swollen under the fur. During the day, he had found two sticks to use as splints, but none of the vines that grew so freely in the summer to tie them with. The boy still didn't know what to use, or if the macaque would even let him touch it.

Ryuu glanced around the canyon. It was blocked on three sides by steep, rocky cliffs. The wall at the back was where he had descended from the night before. The wind had obscured his skid marks, but the mound of snow at the bottom gave it away. The fourth side, where he had trekked that day, opened gently onto a field that overlooked the mountains. In the bright, late-afternoon sunlight, the snowy landscape was blindingly white.

Ryuu lifted the tangerines out of the water. The ice was gone, but the fruit remained crisp. He approached the macaque calmly, with a tangerine extended. Ryuu swore that the saru smiled at him before snatching the fruit. The boy dressed while the snow monkey devoured its treat, then sat down next to it on the bank with his own tangerine. The animal looked at him so hopefully that he broke his tangerine in half to share.

When they finished dinner, Ryuu laid back on the shore to stare at the clouds above him. The snow monkey joined him, pushing itself against the boy to preserve body heat. For the first time in his life, Ryuu felt love. It moved him to tears, but he was careful not to disturb his macaque. He stayed motionless, thinking about how to care for his newfound friend.

Ryuu knew that they would not survive long on the meager selection of food around them, and that his snow monkey's arm needed to be splinted soon. He sadly realized that he would have to go back to town. He had no money, but he was small and fast. Ryuu figured he could steal what they needed easily in the morning rush and make it back to the hot spring before nightfall. He was terrified about being caught and facing the consequences of his schoolyard actions, but he could not let his macaque down.

He also needed to build them a shelter. The ravine provided relief from the wind, and the hot spring made the temperature bearable, but another snowstorm would surely come soon. They needed a roof and walls to survive it. Before he could think farther, Ryuu fell asleep cuddling his snow monkey. Even in Hell's Valley he was content just to have a friend.

Ryuu and the macaque awoke early the next morning. He thawed three more tangerines in the water, offering two of them. The saru took them without hesitation. The boy ate the third tangerine and some Goma seeds. He studied the sky as he chewed.

It was overcast, but Ryuu saw no threatening clouds on the horizon. He knew that the town was southwest of the forest, and the field was facing the rising sun, glowing behind the mist. To get back, he would have to go the opposite direction he had taken the previous day. He knew he couldn't climb the steep ravine wall, so he would have to circle back around the exterior of the peak before descending. It would be a hard trip, but he was determined to succeed.

Before starting out that morning, Ryuu petted his little macaque and promised to return that night. He left two more tangerines and another handful of fern root and then set out. Each step through the deep snow was difficult, but his body was light enough to only sink several inches. An adult would sink to the waist.

It took an hour to make his way around the mountain, carefully erecting stick pyramids to lead him back. When he thought he was on the southwest side, he finally began his descent. It was an arduous journey, but he made his way to the outskirts of town by noon. Only a couple of small, traditional homes speckled the hills outside of town. Ryuu was sure to stay out of sight, but doubted anyone would notice him. He grabbed a bag from a bench on one of the properties he passed.

Once in town, Ryuu scurried down the streets, hiding in doorways and behind stalls. His life as a nobody made hiding his existence easy, and before long, he had gathered everything he needed. The bag was full of fruits and vegetables, as well as nuts and grains. He had even managed to steal several sushi rolls and a long, silk scarf to tie his monkey's splint.

Ryuu made his way out of town cautiously, but ran freely when he reached the hillside. As he sprinted through a field, a farmer who was searching for his missing bag noticed him. Earlier that morning the farmer had heard all about the boy who'd assaulted the headmaster's son. The whole town was searching for the youngster, but he had not been found in two days. The farmer considered marching to town to sound the alarm, but he was too curious. Instead, he put on his coat and boots, and set out after the child.

Ryuu scrambled over the snow and up the mountain as quickly as he could. By following his stick pyramids and tracks, he found his way back. The snow monkey was lounging in the hot spring when he arrived, its arm still grotesquely twisted. He offered it some nuts and berries then joined it in the water. The journey had frozen Ryuu to the bone, but seeing his macaque content warmed him to the soul.

Twenty minutes later, Ryuu and the monkey retreated to the shore. The boy dressed quickly, afraid he would not finish their shelter before nightfall. The clouds had become darker, and the air smelled like snow. The boy started by gathering several large branches and limbs. He stacked them together to create walls and packed the snow in between like mortar. He left a small entry in the front wall.

When the walls were solid, Ryuu placed several straight bamboo shoots across the top, making a roof. He tried to pack snow into the crevices, but it kept falling through. He saw nothing that would make a solid surface, so he focused instead on the snow monkey's broken arm.

The animal was resting near him, interested in his building activities. When he approached, it did not withdraw. Ryuu sat next it, stroking its head for several minutes, before collecting the splint and scarf. The silk scarf was nearly two-feet wide and six-feet long. He tore off a strip, tossing the rest aside. Then he gave the saru a few shoots of Itadori, a natural pain reliever.

When the macaque had finished eating, Ryuu took its arm as gently as he could. The animal whimpered, but did not pull back. He could feel the broken bone through the skin and fur and knew that the ends were not aligned. Before he could lose his nerve, Ryuu pulled the two ends of the bone, twisted, and released, praying that it had set. The saru cried out, but did not run away.

Ryuu studied the animal's arm, hopeful, then placed the sticks on either side, with the silk underneath. Carefully, he splinted the macaque's arm, immobilizing it. After he tied the silk tight, he gave his primate a persimmon, and then he used the rest of the scarf to weave in between the shoots on the roof. It wasn't enough fabric, so he stripped off his shirt to complete it.

The boy was so involved in his work, he never knew that he was being watched. High on the ridge above him, an astounded farmer had seen everything. Although the man wanted to see more, the coming storm drove him back down the mountain, his mind reeling. The deep snow was nearly impassible, and the farmer struggled to get home in time.

The first flakes began to fall as Ryuu tied down the silk scarf on the roof. He quickly packed a layer of snow on top, to insulate the small shelter. Then he and his macaque curled inside. Their combined body heat warmed the shelter quickly, and Ryuu removed his coat to use as a pillow. He fell asleep that night warm and comfortable.

The farmer did not fall asleep as easily. After hiking back down the mountain, the man fed his livestock and prepared supper, all the while thinking about the amazing relationship between the boy and the snow monkey. He had never known the saru to interact with humans, and some even believed the macaques were Oni or demons. Neither the boy nor the snow monkey seemed evil to him. Their interaction looked like benevolence and love in its purest form.

The farmer went to town early the following morning with a shopping list. The market was always loud, but this morning it was deafening. The venders and customers were yelling about a series of thefts the day before.

"It must have that boy Ryuu. He attacked the headmaster's son!"

"I hear he nearly killed the boy!"

"Then he just up and disappeared. The orphanage says that they haven't seen him."

"No-one has seen him, but I bet he's the one that stole fruit from me yesterday."

"He took one of my scarves!"

"He stole from me too!"

"He's a thief! The police are looking for him. He'll get what he deserves!"

The farmer did not say a word. From Mr. Hayashi, he purchased one pair of boy's pants; one small, long-sleeve shirt; one set of children's long johns; one pack of thick socks; a hat and gloves set; and a pair of snow boots in size 1. From Mrs. Konishi, he purchased a thick tatami mat and a new blanket. Finally, he stopped at Mrs. Aoki's stand for a basket of groceries. His odd purchases did not go unnoticed.

"Konnichiwa, Mr. Fujiwara."

"Mrs. Aoki, O-genki desu ka?"

"I'm fine. What unusual things you are buying today."

"Ah yes, gifts for my cousin's son in Nagano. Alas, my tatami needs replacement and my pantry needs to be restocked. Expensive day my friend."

He laughed pleasantly, then bowed politely when he finished his transaction. Mrs. Aoki was too caught up exchanging complaints with the vender next to her to bow back. Mr. Fujiwara headed to the school next. He knew the children would be outside during morning recess, and he was curious about what had happened with Ryuu three days earlier. The commentary he heard in the market did not match the gentle child he saw.

He sat outside the wall, in the shade of a bare cherry tree. Children always spoke freely and loudly, and he hoped he would learn the truth by listening in. Mr. Fujiwara was not disappointed.

"I can't believe Ryuu is still missing."

"Me neither, it's like he disappeared. I hope he's okay."

"I don't! He hit Takeshi right in the face."

"Yeah, after Takeshi hit him with the ice ball first! You all had it coming for pounding him with snowballs."

"Whatever. I'm just glad Takeshi is alright, and I don't care what happens to that worthless orphan."

The farmer slipped away. When he returned home, he packed up the supplies in a large rucksack, then set out for Hell's Valley. The farmer hiked for nearly three hours without seeing a single track or stick pyramid. The snow the night before had hidden them completely. He had hoped to deliver the goods to the boy, but realized sadly that he could not find his way to the spring.

The farmer thought long and hard about his dilemma. He didn't want to take the products back with him, but leaving the bag on the ground would render its contents useless. If it snowed, all the valuable products inside would be lost until spring. Ryuu couldn't wait that long. Finally, the farmer constructed a high tripod of bamboo shoots. He placed the bag on top, nestled between the supports, using another bamboo shoot to reach high enough. Mr. Fujiwara threw the shoot aside, returned home, fed his livestock, ate supper, and slept soundly, convinced that he had done the right thing.

Ryuu never left the hot spring that day. He and the snow monkey spent their time relaxing in the hot water and feasting on the produce he had stolen the day before. The snow had sealed his refuge completely, making it warm and comfortable inside. Outside, without a shirt, Ryuu shivered fiercely whenever he moved away from the hot water or ventured from his fortress. The coat hung loose on him, allowing the cold air to snake up his bare skin.

Ryuu knew that he would need to get more food the following day, but the thought of hiking through the snow made his feet ache and his small frame tremble. The journey was hard, and cold, and stealing a second time would be much harder than stealing the first. The boy wondered what the town would do to him if they caught him. Would he be whipped? Would he be incarcerated? If Takeshi passed away, would they kill him? These thoughts plagued the poor boy all night.

Ryuu awoke in the early morning to the shriek of wind in the trees above. Although his little haven was calm, the winter was fierce beyond the ravine. He could see the snow whipping across the clearing to the east.

He looked at the meager selection of food left from the day before. Little more than a handful of berries and nuts remained. The snow monkey had eaten voraciously as had Ryuu. Years of hunger made self-control difficult. He promised better rationing with his next set of groceries.

The boy cuddled with his macaque before setting out. As soon as he ventured beyond the stone walls, the wind tore through him. He felt like he was naked. The coat did nothing to shield him. By the time the boy had worked his way around the mountain, his feet were frozen, and he was shaking violently. Ryuu stumbled forward, knowing he would never make it as far as the town. Thoughts of his saru propelled him ahead blindly, until at last he fell to the ground, nearly hypothermic.

He looked up at the sky and prayed that he could find the strength for the sake of his friend. Above him, Ryuu saw a large sack wedged between bamboo shoots. He stared at it for several moments, before recognizing it as a bag filled with goods. He stood up, still shivering, and retrieved a long shoot from ground nearby. Using it, he pulled the bag to the ground.

Ryuu was shocked when he opened the satchel. Inside he found clothing, bedding, and food! Everything he needed! He was sure that this meant the deities were pleased with him, and he put on the clothes and coat with renewed vigor. The socks were warm, and the boots were cozy. The hat and gloves were luxuries he had never experienced before. He floated back to the spring on a cloud of ecstasy and adrenaline.

A blizzard hit that night. It raged for two days, leaving behind drifts that were higher than houses. The farmer had hoped to check on Ryuu, but was unable to dig out for several days. He worried incessantly about the small boy trapped in Hell's Valley, and hoped that Ryuu had discovered the supplies. It was nearly a week before Mr. Fujiwara could attempt the mountain journey again.

The farmer set out early in the morning with another large sack filled with food. He made certain to include several fruits, vegetables, nuts, and berries, as well as rice and grilled fish. The air was so cold that the snow had frozen solid. Mr. Fujiwara walked on top of it, slipping often, but not sinking. He made it as far as the tripod in two hours, and decided to go farther this time.

Up the hill, he saw the top of a small stick pyramid. The wind had cleared the area around it. The structure was crude, but the arrangement of sticks pointed to the left. He decided to follow the directions. Mr. Fujiwara did not find another pyramid as he circumnavigated the peak, but he did find the entrance to the hot spring.

He looked around, but saw no shelter or signs of life. He began to think he had stumbled upon the wrong spring, when he heard the frantic cries of a monkey coming from a small hole in a mound of snow. Horrified, the farmer realized that the boy and his macaque had been buried alive. The ice was hard to penetrate, but little by little the farmer dug out the shelter. It took nearly an hour. At last, he was able to see inside.

Ryuu lay motionless on the tatami mat on the floor of his little snow house. The monkey stood beside him, one paw placed protectively on the boy's chest. The farmer could see a slight rise and fall, and thanked the gods that the boy still lived. After a moment of thought, he offered the snow monkey a handful of Gingko nuts. Hesitantly, the macaque accepted the offer, withdrawing to the corner to eat.

The farmer carefully inched into the miniature fortress. The air was stagnant and old, thick with carbon dioxide. Mr. Fujiwara grasped the child under the arms and pulled Ryuu outside. The macaque joined the boy immediately, breathing deeply. The boy inhaled sharply, then coughed out the bitter air. He opened his eyes, but looked around without comprehension. When his eyes settled upon the farmer, he cried out in fear.

"I'm here to help you, Ryuu. Do not worry. I know you are innocent, and this saru knows you are pure. I will not deceive you or turn you over to the authorities."

"Who are you?"

"My name is Mr. Fujiwara. I am a humble farmer honored to offer assistance. Here, stand up and let me help you to the water. I have food for you, too."

Ryuu was confused, but he followed the farmer's instructions. The man helped him undress and get in the spring. The hot water, mixed with the cold oxygen, revived the boy, though he sniffled and coughed heartily. Soon Ryuu's hunger drove him to the shore, where the snow monkey waited anxiously for him. The boy dressed quickly, then sat with his macaque, murmuring words of comfort between sniffles. Mr. Fujiwara served them each food and water, then sat back to allow them to eat.

Still wearing a splint on its arm, the snow monkey grasped food with both hands. The farmer was amazed that the animal had retained control of the limb, and impressed that the young boy had known what to do. He allowed Ryuu to finish his meal before asking questions.

"How did you know what to do for the snow monkey?"

"We had no toys at the orphanage, so I brought books home from the school library every night. By the end of first grade, I had read all the text from the school library, so I started to borrow books from Dr. Miyasaki last summer. One of them taught about treating breaks."

Mr. Fujiwara nodded his head in understanding, but frankly was stupefied. At nearly forty, he could barely read and write, yet this seven-year-old in front of him had successfully studied from a medical text. The farmer queried again.

"How did you know how to build your little house over there? You didn't learn that in a medical book or in the school library."

"The maintenance man who gave me my shoes often talked about his adventures from his younger days. He taught me about edible plants, marking paths, and building shelters."

Listening to the young boy, Mr. Fujiwara felt wave after wave of reverence. Somehow this child had survived ten days in one of the harshest climates on earth, and saved a snow monkey in the process, using only his wits. The child hacked viciously, his forehead covered in sweat. The farmer took the boy's hands in his own, and looked him carefully in the eyes.

"Ryuu, please come stay at my house at the base of the mountain. It is not safe for you to stay here. I promise I will not turn you in."

"Thank you, sir, but I can't leave Saru here alone."

The farmer thought a moment. Bringing a child into his household was a huge step, but adding a monkey on top of it seemed insurmountable. Before he could answer, a furry, splinted arm rested on his leg. The snow monkey looked Mr. Fujiwara straight in the eyes. The farmer bowed.

"Please Ryuu, bring it with you."

Mr. Fujiwara gathered up the supplies from the campsite and packed everything into the two bags. The old scarf and shirt were buried too deep to salvage, but Ryuu climbed into his fortress to grab the tatami and new blanket. Mr. Fujiwara led the way back around the mountain. Ryuu, swaying from fever, and Saru, running circles, followed behind.

It was sunset, when the odd group finally exited the mountain forest and arrived at the small house. The farmer was relieved to get home, but the boy and the monkey became increasingly anxious as they approached. Ryuu feared that the farmer was leading him to capture, and the macaque had never ventured out of the forest before. The boy and monkey held hands, like siblings.

Ryuu and Saru remained outside while the farmer went in the house to turn on the lights and start a fire. They sat together on the bench near the barn, leaning into each other for support. In the distance, Ryuu could see the town lights glowing. Between sniffles and coughs, he wondered if Dr. Miyasaki had been able to help Takeshi. His guilt weighed heavily on him.

The farmer exited his house and joined the boy on the bench, careful not to frighten the snow monkey. He gave Ryuu a large cup of hot tea and a plate of tempura. To the snow monkey, he provided several large Kuri chestnuts and a Fuji apple. Both little creatures ate silently.

"Do you want to come into the house Ryuu?"

"I don't think Saru would be comfortable inside, sir. May we stay in the barn instead please?"

"Of course. Give me a minute and I will help you set up."

The farmer went inside, returning a moment later with an armful of extra blankets. He cleared an area for the boy and the macaque in an empty stall. He laid the tatami on top of a mound of hay to make it more comfortable and spread a couple of large quilts to protect the child from scratches. Ryuu's eyes were glassy, and his cough produced dark mucous, but he lay down gratefully in the barn with his monkey. He had never been more comfortable in his life.

Early the following morning, the farmer found Ryuu delirious from fever. Mr. Fujiwara used snow to help control the boy's temperature, but he realized quickly that Ryuu needed immediate medical care. The farmer could not risk taking the boy to town, but perhaps he could convince Dr. Miyasaki to come to his farm.

The farmer nodded politely at the street venders as he passed through the market that day. As usual, the venders were busy discussing recent events. He listened carefully as he strolled by.

"Good thing Takeshi is alright. His father was so upset that he tried to hunt down rotten Ryuu the first night, but the wind hid the trail and made it impossible to track."

"I hear that the police haven't found as much as a foot print yet. I wonder where that boy went."

"The orphanage hasn't seen hide nor hair of him. He didn't even come back for his mat. They've already given his things to the other children."

"Some people think he went to Hell's Valley."

"It's been over a week, if he did go there, he has surely perished."

Mr. Fujiwara continued on his way. Within moments, he stood in front of the medical clinic. The receptionist smiled brightly when he entered.

"Konnichiwa Mr. Fujiwara. Do you have an appointment today?"

"No, but I need to speak with Dr. Miyasaki please."

"Certainly. Please have a seat."

Mr. Fujiwara waited patiently, thinking about Ryuu and the snow monkey. He could take care of the boy's immediate needs, but sooner or later the authorities would take notice and discover the boy. It would be at least two more months before spring, and Ryuu could not live outside, or in a barn, for the rest of the winter. The saru also needed to be considered. It needed to return to the forest soon. Dr. Miyasaki's booming voice pulled the farmer to his feet.

"Good morning, Mr. Fujiwara. Please, come to my office."

"Good morning, Dr. Miyasaki. Thank you for seeing me."

The two men settled into the office, exchanging pleasantries. Dr. Miyasaki was surprised to see Mr. Fujiwara. The farmer only came to the clinic in dire emergencies, like when his wife had her accident. He was clearly in good health, so his visit must be for someone else. The doctor closed the door for privacy.

"So, tell me Mr. Fujiwara, what brings you to me today?"

"I need your help at my farm, sir."

"You're not sick, so who is?"

"I'd rather show you sir, but please, bring your medical bag."

The two men had known each other since the farmer was a boy, and the doctor was new to the practice of medicine. Although Mr. Fujiwara was not highly-educated, he was highly respected and known for his honesty, decency, and self-sufficiency. Dr. Miyasaki often purchased the farmer's produce and considered the man a friend.

"As you wish. I will come to your farmstead at 2:00 this afternoon."

"Domo arigatou gozaimasu."

Mr. Fujiwara bowed deeply before leaving the clinic. On his way back through the market, he picked up miso soup, tonkatsu, strawberries, and ramen. He was home by noon.

Ryuu was asleep in the barn when the farmer returned, but the snow monkey was shrieking loudly as it leapt from one upright to another. The farmer placed a pile of strawberries on the mat near the boy. Within moments, the snow monkey had calmed enough to eat its treat, both paws grasping hungrily at the berries. The silk holding on its splint was ragged, but still in place.

The farmer sat down in the barn and ate a small meal from his market purchases. Ryuu moaned often, but did not awaken. His small body trembled under the blankets, but his face was red with fever. Mr. Fujiwara prayed that the doctor would not be delayed.

At promptly 2:00, Dr. Miyasaki crested the hill. The farmer was waiting outside for him. The doctor was a little surprised when Mr. Fujiwara led him to the barn instead of to the house, but he was completely shocked to find Ryuu and the snow monkey.

"What in the Kami do we have here? Mr. Fujiwara, are you harboring a fugitive?"

"I suppose that is what they call it, sir. I found the boy in Hell's Valley. He needs your help."

The doctor debated a moment. He felt a civic duty to report the incident immediately, but he felt a moral obligation to provide medical care. His eyes rested on the monkey, and on the makeshift splint.

"Is that your saru, Mr. Fujiwara? Did you splint its arm?"

"No sir, that is Ryuu's snow monkey. He doesn't know it, but I watched him care for the macaque the second day after his disappearance. I was so astounded, I decided not to report him. I returned yesterday, found him buried from the blizzard, and brought him here."

"I see. How did he know how to care for the break?"

"From the books you gave him, sir."

Dr. Miyasaki stared at the farmer in disbelief. Although the doctor had provided the books, he thought the boy was just looking at the pictures. He never imagined that the child could read and understand the words. As intelligent as the doctor was, he had been unable to understand that bone text until he was a teenager. Applying the information took years of practice.

"Why did the macaque allow him to do it?"

"I don't know, sir. They seem to have a spirit connection."

Many people believed that the mountain Kami could take multiple forms, and often traveled as a snow monkey. Sometimes the Kami were evil, like Oni or demons; other times they were benevolent. Looking at the beautiful animal protecting the sick little boy, the doctor couldn't help but feel there was something special about both of them.

"I will treat him, and I will not report you, but Ryuu will need to face what he has done soon. Takeshi was badly hurt, and that type of assault cannot be ignored, Mr. Fujiwara."

"True, Dr. Miyasaki, but Ryuu only threw the ice back after being hit by Takeshi first."

"How do you know that, Mr. Fujiwara?"

"I listened to the children, sir. They all know what really happened."

Dr. Miyasaki didn't reply, but his mind began reconsidering his condemnation of the boy before him. Like everyone else in town, Dr. Miyasaki had believed that Ryuu's actions were unprovoked and malicious. As he examined the boy, he found a crusted scab across his cheek, in the middle stages of healing.

"Mr. Fujiwara, did this injury happen from the snow storm?"

"No sir, that injury is from Takeshi's ice a week ago."

The doctor did not ask any more questions. He woke Ryuu and provided medicine for the fever, tended the wound on his cheek, and washed the dirt from his body. He gave the farmer extra medicine for the boy, and a new splint and bandage for the monkey. The macaque never left Ryuu's side. Before departing, Dr. Miyasaki spoke outside with the farmer.

"Mr. Fujiwara, you have told me many things today that contradict the public narrative. I need to do some research, but I respect what you are doing for Ryuu and will not betray your trust in me."

The two men bowed before the doctor headed back to town. The farmer finished his chores, gave Ryuu a second dose of medication and some hot noodles, fed his livestock and the snow money, and settled in for the night. He was glad that Dr. Miyasaki had been open minded, and was relieved that he had at least one friend who might hopefully become an ally.

The following morning, Ryuu was still coughing, but his fever had dropped and his appetite returned. After breakfast, the boy replaced his snow monkey's splint with the materials the doctor had left. Afterwards, Ryuu and Saru spent a few hours outside, taking care to remain in the tree line and out of view.

The boy and his macaque both ate a large lunch and then napped until Mr. Fujiwara brought them dinner in the barn. The farmer sat on the ground with them to eat. Ryuu ate quietly at first, but he had too many questions to remain silent.

"Sir, do you think the doctor will tell the police I am here?"

"No Ryuu, I do not think so."

"Sir, do you think I could go to the hot spring tomorrow for Saru?"

"Let's see how you feel in the morning, ok? If you are up for the trip, and the weather is decent, then we can go together."

"Sir, why are you helping me?"

"Because you deserve it Ryuu."

Never in his life, had Ryuu felt he deserved anything more than the nothing he got. He never felt he was worthy of love, entitled to material goods, or meritorious of attention. He never felt like his presence should be acknowledged or that his needs ought to be met. It moved the boy to tears to be cared about, and he sobbed heartily.

The farmer sat on one side of Ryuu, stroking the boy's back, while Saru sat on the other, touching his leg. Sandwiched between them, Ryuu felt like he was part of a real family. He spoke through tears.

"I am in your debt, sir. I will never forget what you are doing for me, and I will devote my life to paying you back for your assistance."

"No Ryuu, I am the one who is indebted. Since my wife died, I have been unable to care about anyone. My spirit was frozen with grief, and although I was breathing, I was not living. Dear boy, you have melted my heart and thawed my soul."

That night the farmer slept in the house and the boy stayed in the barn with his monkey. Ryuu could still feel the farmer's consoling pats on his back, and Mr. Fujiwara could still feel his heart break at the boy's tears. They both had rediscovered the treasure of love and family.

The morning dawned clear, and Ryuu awoke fever-free. As promised, the farmer accompanied the boy and his snow monkey back to the hot spring. All three enjoyed the excursion. They lounged in the hot water, dined together on the shore, and watched the clouds pass overhead. When they returned to the farmstead, both Mr. Fujiwara and Ryuu felt completely relaxed. They never saw the group hiding in the trees until they were well across the field.

Ryuu, Saru, and the farmer stood still as the group of men approached them. In the lead was Dr. Miyasaki, followed by the police chief, the headmaster from the school, and the director of the orphanage. Mr. Fujiwara's face dropped and Ryuu began to tremble, but the doctor nodded reassuringly before beginning his speech.

"Gentlemen, as you know, Ryuu is accused of assault, theft, evading police, and failing to return to the orphanage. I have fulfilled my duty and alerted you of his whereabouts, but now I must stand against you in his defense."

Dr. Miyasaki stood between the boy and Mr. Fujiwara to face the authorities. The police captain looked surprised and the director looked confused. The headmaster was furious. His face turned a bright shade of red, and his expression of shock and hatred seared into the small boy. Spittle shot from his lips as he spoke.

"Dr. Miyasaki, what is the meaning of this? You took care of Takeshi, you know how serious his injury was. My boy could have died! How dare you stand up for this miscreant!"

"I stand for truth and justice. Ryuu did hit Takeshi with the ice, but only after your son attacked him first. The scar on Ryuu's cheek is evidence, and the school children admitted the events to me when I conducted the school physicals yesterday."

The headmaster sputtered but turned away. He knew the truth about what had happened that day but did not want to publicly acknowledge his son's bad behavior. The police captain took over the proceedings, careful to protect the headmaster's interests.

"Be that as it may, we still have an issue, Dr. Miyasaki. Ryuu may not return to school under the circumstances."

"That is not an issue sir. I will tutor the child myself in the evenings. He has shown incredible intelligence and aptitude. It would be my pleasure to take on his education."

"That's fine, doctor, but we also have the issue of theft. He stole over forty yen of product."

The doctor retrieved his billfold. Annoyed, the police captain nodded consent to payment. The headmaster also begrudgingly agreed with a slight bow. The orphanage director, however, was not satisfied.

"Gentleman, it is very kind of Dr. Miyasaki to take responsibility for Ryuu's education and to pay restitution, but the boy no longer has a place in the orphanage here. He must be sent to Tokyo where there are sufficient funding and supplies for his care. The snow monkey will not be tolerated."

Mr. Fujiwara looked at Ryuu. The small boy was shaking, holding onto Saru like a child cuddling a stuffed toy. For the first time since they entered the field, the timid farmer felt emboldened. If Dr. Miyasaki could stand up to the police and to the headmaster, then he could face the director. His voice was quiet and polite, but firm and decisive.

"Sir, I will adopt Ryuu. He can live here with me, and care for his monkey. The orphanage need not concern itself any longer. I would be pleased to sign paperwork at your convenience."

The director's eyes flew wide. He knew that every adoption included a managerial bonus. The money would not go amiss in his pockets, and having Ryuu out of the way opened additional space and funding for new recruits. He nodded and smiled brightly.

"Very well! I will draw up paperwork tonight and you can sign tomorrow."

A light snow began falling, and the authorities quickly said their farewells before hurrying back to town. Dr. Miyasaki alone remained with the farmer and the boy. Together, the trio entered the barn and settled onto the hay. The saru lay on Ryuu's lap, listening to the doctor's voice.

"I am sorry to have frightened you this evening. When the police captain questioned me this afternoon, he had already gathered significant information from the market venders. I decided it was best to be honest. I did not want to give you away, but I could not lie. All I could do was stand in your defense."

"All is well, friend, but I am unsure how to pay you for tutoring Ryuu and for the goods. I will begin selling my possessions immediately."

"Pay me, Mr. Fujiwara? I will teach Ryuu for free and he will work at the clinic to pay off his debt. He should be at my office at three tomorrow. He will help me with patients in the afternoon and will study in the evenings. In this way he can spend the daylight hours caring for his macaque and helping you. Agreed?"

The farmer and the boy both nodded excitedly. They walked the doctor to the end of the farmstead, bowed deeply, and then turned back through the snow. Although Ryuu had not spoken once since they returned that day, he finally found his voice.

"You really want to adopt me, Mr. Fujiwara?"

"Yes Ryuu, I truly do."

"May I call you papa?"

"Nothing would make me happier son."

That night, Ryuu and Saru ventured into Mr. Fujiwara's house for the first time. The farmer led them to a small room in the back furnished with a futon and separated by a fusuma panel. Although they were humble accommodations, to the boy it seemed like nirvana. Ryuu slept soundly, and woke up early to clean the house for his papa. When the farmer awoke at sunrise, the boy had already finished most of the chores.

Ryuu spent the day at the hot spring with his snow monkey, and then reported to Dr. Miyasaki at three. He worked at the clinic, then studied hard at night. Each day thereafter was the same. He had never been happier in his entire life.

By the end of the winter, Ryuu had settled into his routine and Saru's arm had healed. In late April, Mr. Fujiwara, Ryuu, and the macaque made one final journey together to the hot spring. They played in the water, picnicked together, and even foraged for fresh stalks and parsley. The snow monkey was livelier than ever, and seemed especially excited when they visited the back side of the peak. Ryuu had never been there before, but Mr. Fujiwara knew of a path that led to a hidden valley.

As they approached the hollow, Saru began to shriek and grunt. Ryuu had never heard it make those sounds before, and he worried that his friend was ill. He turned to pick up his snow monkey, but the primate dashed ahead into the forest.

Ryuu and Mr. Fujiwara followed the animal quietly. When they passed through the trees, they entered a small clearing. In front of them were a dozen snow monkeys, all stroking and caressing Ryuu's macaque. The little animal chirped and chortled, elated to have found its family.

Ryuu looked sadly at the reunion. He knew it was best for his macaque to rejoin the troop, but he had fervently wished to keep his friend to himself forever. Mr. Fujiwara patted the boy's shoulder. Ryuu realized that he had something even better than a friend, he had a father. He and the farmer walked home in peace.

The next years flew by for Ryuu. He worked hard on the farm and studied diligently with Dr. Miyasaki. Every day he made the trip to the hot spring. Most times he just sat quietly reading, but sometimes he saw his little macaque. Saru always sat on his lap and dug through his pockets for treats. Occasionally the entire troop would join him. Ryuu loved their company. When his snow monkeys returned to their home in the forest, he went home to his.

Ryuu felt that he was the luckiest boy alive. He had the world's kindest papa, the finest teacher, and the best animal friends in the world. Even in the harshest winter weather, his heart was always warm. He might not be popular or affluent, but he was certainly beloved.

Jagged icicles,
Dangling from cardiac eaves,
Vaporized by love.

Silent Night

Silent night, wholly
Chaste in a lace negligee
Of snow. All is white.

Nor 'easter

A nor'easter blew
The violent storm all feared
The forecast was true

COOPERSMITH'S

David W. Dutton

SANDWICHED BETWEEN WT GRANTS and JC Penny on North Walnut Street in Milford, sat southern Delaware's premier ladies shop. Or should I say *shoppe*?

Regardless, Coopersmith's was the store that most fashionable women frequented in the late 1950s and early 60s. It was on a par with John Wanamaker's in Wilmington and The Blum Store in Philadelphia. They carried only the best, and their prices reflected that fact.

It was a few days before Christmas when my father and I ventured forth to find a suitable present for my mother. She was out, playing bridge, so it was the perfect time for us to sneak off. Dad parked his battered pick-up truck on the east side of Walnut Street, a few spaces down from the store.

The double-glass doors were set far back from the sidewalk, accessible via a gently sloped, tile ramp. On either side, large glass display windows exhibited the treasures to be found inside. Each window held three mannequins sporting the latest in fashion. Around their feet were displayed an abundance of other "essential" products: bags, sweaters, scarves, perfume, jewelry. It was a veritable wonderland of feminine mystique.

As my father and I walked toward the front doors, I stopped him mid-way and pointed to one of the mannequins to our left.

The mannequin wore a quilted, red velvet robe with clustered rhinestone buttons from the neck to hem. The collar and cuffs were soft, brown mink.

"Mom really liked that."

My father smiled. "Knowing your mother, I'm sure she did. Can't you see you mother cooking bacon in that?" My father laughed and gave me a playful push.

I laughed too. The thought was ludicrous.

My mother loved fine things, especially fine clothes. Coopersmith's was one of her favorite haunts. I had been with her when she priced the robe. It cost an astounding ninety dollars. I guess the mink drove the price up.

Dad held the door open for me and followed me into the store. The overpowering scent of perfume assailed our nostrils. It was a smell that I had always loved, one that I can still remember today.

As we stood surveying the array spread before us, an older woman in a severe black dress approached us. Her narrow reading glasses sat on the end of her nose, anchored by a chain that encircled her neck. She paused for a moment, her watery blue eyes looking over the top of her spectacles as she surveyed my father.

"Can I help you?" Her voice held a subtle note of disdain.

My father was an impressive man, slightly over six feet with sandy hair and hazel eyes. The clerk wasn't seeing those features. She was seeing the old, canvas hunting jacket, the plaid flannel shirt, the dark-green Dickies brand work pants, and the battered work boots. When dressed as a gentleman, my father cut quite a figure. I had seen him in a tuxedo several times, but there was no need to try to explain that to the clerk who stood in front of us. She had already made up her mind.

My father gave her his best smile, which weakened her a little. "I'm looking for a sweater for my wife."

"Oh, a sweater. What did you have in mind?"

"A cardigan. Cashmere."

Her pencil-thin eyebrows arched. "Cashmere?"

My father smiled again. "Yes."

"We have several. Please follow me." She turned. We did as instructed.

The clerk led us through a maze of tables and racks to a glass display case near the back of the store. There she stopped and indicated the row of sweaters within.

"We display them this way because we don't want people finger-ing them." She looked at my father. "I'm sure you understand."

My father nodded. "Certainly."

"I'll be glad to show them to you. What size does your wife wear?"

"A seven, dress size."

The clerk nodded sagely. "Then a small will be perfect. Of course, we have them in all sizes."

My father nodded again. "Certainly."

"Do you see something you like?"

My father and I studied the sweaters. They were all white with pearl buttons. Beyond that, each was different. Beads, pearls, rhine-stones, ribbons, and lace in a variety of colors decorated the various garments. It was mind-boggling.

Finally, my father turned to me and laid his hand on my shoul-der. "What do you think, Sport?"

I smiled and pointed to the one I liked. Its neckline and plackets were decorated with tiny, frosted beads in soft shades of blue, green, and pink. These were grouped as if they were bouquets and accented with pearls and delicate silver leaves. "That one."

"I like that one, too." My father turned to clerk and smiled. "We'll have that one."

The clerk nodded, opened the rear of the display case, and with-drew the sweater.

"Very nice selection. I think your wife will be very pleased." She closed the case and led us to the checkout desk. She laid the sweater on the desk and looked at my father.

"That will be eighteen dollars and seventy-five cents. Cash or charge?" She spoke the last word as if it would be highly unlikely. She was right.

My father opened his wallet and handed her a twenty-dollar bill. She thanked him, procured a dollar twenty-five in change, and began enfolding the sweater in reams of tissue paper before placing it in a box.

"Would you like us to wrap this for you?"

My father smiled. "That would be nice."

Southern Delaware in the late 1950s tried to keep up with all the new trends and styles. However, in some areas, we remained traditionalists. Christmas wrapping was one of those areas. Red, green, and gold were the norm, though occasionally blue and silver found its way beneath the tree.

In a few minutes, the clerk returned with our package. The glossy, Pepto Bismol pink wrapping was shocking. The olive green ribbon and bow did little to soften the blow.

The clerk looked at my father and actually smiled. "Isn't this lovely? The colors are so *today*."

My father nodded. "Yes, ma'am. Very nice. Thank you."

She slipped the present into a bag and handed it to my father. Then she smiled again. "Have a merry Christmas."

My father smiled back. "You do the same."

Christmas morning arrived on schedule. I sat at the kitchen table while my mother fried bacon and eggs in a cast iron skillet. My father had accepted the arduous task of preparing toast for three people using a toaster that only had one slot.

Once breakfast was behind us, we moved to the living room and began opening presents. The tree was beautiful in its corner. A blue spruce with multicolored glass balls and lights–and icicles. Had to have icicles. I had lobbied long and hard for a traditional tree. For the last several years, my mother's idea of sophistication had been for my father to purchase a short-needled spruce and then paint it silver. On Christmas Eve, "Santa Claus" would decorate it with blue lights and blue and red glass balls. A lighted star with a red border would grace the top. My mother loved it, but I thought it severe and cold. At least that chapter was now behind us.

I was assigned the job of distributing the gifts. It was the one way to keep my fidgeting in check. Midway through the ceremony of boxes, paper, and bows, my father looked over at me.

"Why don't you give your mother that gift I hid behind the tree?"

I returned a knowing wink and dug through the remaining packages until I found the present. Slowly I withdrew the gaudy, pink and olive creation. I looked at it for a moment and then handed it to my mother.

I smiled at her. "This is from Dad."

My father laughed. "Well, you helped pick it out, so, if she doesn't like it, you're as much at fault as I am."

My mother took the present and smiled. "I'm sure I'll love it." She studied the box for a second and then looked up at my father. "Where did this come from?"

He laughed and shook his head. "'I'll never tell. You'll have to open it to find out."

Removing the ribbon and tearing aside the pink paper, my mother exposed the top of the box. The turquoise script announcing Coopersmith's reached from one corner of the lid to the other. My mother laughed. "Only Coopersmith's could get away with that wrapping paper."

"I wanted to re-wrap it, but Dad wouldn't let me."

"No way in hell! For what it cost, I wanted you to get the full effect."

Gently laying aside the tissue paper, my mother held the sweater up in front of her. For a moment, she was speechless. "Well, this is beautiful." She rubbed a sleeve against her cheek. "And so soft."

My father beamed. "Cashmere."

"I know that, silly. You shouldn't have. It's too much."

"Only the best for our girl, right, Sport?"

"Right, Dad."

Christmas is like that–full of silly little memories that come to mean so much as one grows older. The sweater, with its pink and olive wrapping, was but one of many that I hold dear. Coopersmith's is long since gone, but the remembrance of that Christmas will never fade away.

Snowflakes in the Air

Cold winds whipped the air
Blowing snowflakes in my face
On my tongue light landings

Heat

Ocean waves part legs
lifting ice cold tiara
to reveal heat source.

BLACKBERRY WINTER

Dianne Pearce

THERE HAD ALWAYS BEEN SOMETHING contrary about Margaret. She seemed to be patently incapable of doing what was good for her. For example, she boasted quite the scar on her chin from trying to reach a kite stuck in their front tree when she was eight, because even though her father had said he would lift her up to reach it, she knew she could do it on her own, and had climbed up on a TV tray to try before he could help. Of course the tray, designed for nothing heavier than a Hungry-Man TV dinner, collapsed sickeningly under her weight, and her face smashed into the side of the mimosa tree like a battering ram.

In junior high, when no one asked her to the snow dance, Margaret decided she was probably bisexual. Her parents thought she probably wasn't, having known her for quite a few years at this point, but they didn't want to be closed minded, so they gave no more than gentle advice about the shyness of junior high boys. Margaret seemed not to hear them, and began asking other girls from school out on dates, which, after many rejections and being laughed at by both sexes, resulted in her getting felt up and tongue kissed by Jennifer Cugliotti in Mr. Wilson's supply closet. She was never sure if it was the smell of ammonia that permeated the room, or the experience of

Jennifer forcing Margaret's hand into her crotch, but one of the two made Margaret one-hundred percent sure she was not bisexual at all, actually, which, as she told her mom and dad, she had suspected all the time.

When she graduated from high school, against the best advice of everyone who mattered at the time, Margaret decided to become an artist. Her high school art teacher, Mrs. Potts, thought Margaret was as sweet as could be and about as naturally talented as a duck with a broken pencil. Her parents loved her artistic nature and general verve dearly, but found themselves in close agreement with Mrs. Potts. All three attempted, as kindly as they could, to convince her that "making art" was not something that Margaret could do and expect results in terms of acclaim and sales. However, although Margaret had passed her state-mandated hearing test every year from K-12, she was inexplicably deaf on this point.

Margaret began her artistic journey in college with oils, using large palette knives, instead of brushes or even the more ergonomic and delicate painting knives, to spread the paint thickly and randomly on canvas or salvaged pieces of dirty wood. She was, it must be said, less interested in expressing anything through her art than she was in the feel of the wooden handle in her hand, the slap the paint made when it hit canvas or board, the squirmy feeling she got in her spine when she pushed her pinky into the paint to sign her name on her work, and the way she looked in her splattered overalls, hair tied in a literal knot on the side of her head, palette knife in her teeth as she squeezed more paint onto her latest creation. She really looked and felt like an artist; why shouldn't she be one? As she tended to ignore or not "get" the instruction of her art professors, each thickly coated painting she finished resembled more a cheese board at the end of a party than a masterwork. In fact, instructors and friends often re-marked that Margaret's work made them feel hunger more than any-thing else. She did sell a few pieces at her senior show, but, without exception, all were purchased by maître d'hotels, who thought only that her work would increase the appetites of their patrons. Still, her loving parents paid for the degree, and so Margaret graduated.

A few years later, sitting in a studio full of what appeared to be an endless supply of canvas serving trays that needed the day-old brie scraped off of them, she realized that her genius was invisible to others. As she had been raised to believe that a person could get an A for effort, Margaret was more than a little downtrodden to find that this was incorrect. She picked up all but her favorite piece, and carried them to the freight elevator in the rehabbed warehouse that served as studio and home, and carted them down and out to the curb, and heaped them next to the broken canvas stretchers and smashed pottery of her fellow tenants. Margaret returned to her studio, propped her one remaining piece on an easel (*Dawn Over Echo Pond*, which looked as if it should have been named *Egg-Over-Easy-ish*) and stood in front of it to snap a selfie of herself. Then she walked into her bathroom, and in the light of the too-bright bulb hanging above the old mirrored medicine cabinet that was shedding its silvering at an alarming rate, she took a pair of scissors and cut off her hair at the knot. Margaret shook her head, and her hair stuck out around her in an undelicate hallow of mismatched lengths. She again lifted the scissors, and began cutting and cutting, until her hair was, at the long spots, two inches from her scalp, and, in some spots, down to the white of her head. The pile of hair on the floor almost tempted her to resume painting, as all that hair would be a killer addition to a mixed-media work, and would certainly help dispel thoughts of food when people looked at it. Instead, she swept it away with her old straw broom, like a witch who'd lost her powers, and phoned her friend Callie to see if she wanted to go for a drink.

Mrs. Potts was correct, Margaret was both as talented as a duck with a broken pencil, and as sweet as can be. She had a very kind and gentle way with children, animals, homeless people, waitresses, you name it. Margaret needed a job, of course, and luckily Callie had gotten her degree in the much more practical field of early childhood education, and so was able to help Margaret secure a part-time job teaching art in a K-5 Montessori school. Her slightly messy way of dress combined with her kooky hair only convinced the wealthy parents who sent their children to the school that Margaret was the real deal, and that they were lucky to have her. The children adored her. They all were talented, lovely, brilliant, sweet angels in her eyes. She began to wonder if perhaps teaching wasn't her true art form.

And so it was that once Margaret was done being an artist, and ventured outside of her studio, to drink lattes in coffee shops, to teach small children, to meet with friends for after-work drinks. She found herself sought-after company by Callie, and no small amount of single men. In her usual blind way, Margaret assumed the new-found attention was due not to her being sweet and finally available in the world, but to her new haircut. Therefore, each time she noticed even one little group of hairs attempting to grow longer she instantly re-chopped them none-too-artfully with her scissors. The interest of eligible men continued despite her patchy hair, but Margaret could not seem to find one that she felt a "vibe" with, until the one day, as the second grade kids in her last class were being picked up one at a time by their nannies, she met Stephan.

Stephan was the unmarried uncle of Kennedy, one of Margaret's favorite children because of her red hair and splattery ways with paint. He found himself instantly taken by Margaret's very delicate features beneath her concentration camp hair. Stephan simply assumed Margaret's horrible hair was the result of a run-in with lice from all the little kids she worked with, and so was able to ignore it. While Kennedy pulled at his hand, whining, "Uncle Stephan, look at this!" Stephan wasted no time asking for Margaret's name, her number, and her next free day to have coffee. Margaret ended up leaving school and hopping in his BMW with him and Kennedy. They took Kennedy home where Stephan's sister was thrilled to see him with the "totally legit" art teacher, and then he took Margaret for drinks and apps.

As they walked back to his car after dinner, Stephan wound his hand into the scarf she wore loose around her neck, and pulled her face into his for a kiss. It was a move more lusty than aggressive, and just like that, Stephan became a fixture in the old art studio Margaret still called home, cuddling his large form around her through the nights on the second-hand mattress that served as a bed, a sofa, and a kitchen table, his many tailored suits hanging from the empty easels like some new form of art. Luckily he also happened to have a key to the place, and let himself in one evening just as Margaret was about to chop away at her growing hair, and so was finally able to put a stop to that practice, as he told her that as much as her crazy haircut had not attracted him when they met, her sweet face had drawn in him, and he had, of course, counted on her hair growing back from whatever misfortune had befallen her. Margaret was dumbfounded to realize that Stephan hadn't been attracted to her because of her haircut. Once again the story she told herself about herself was incorrect, but she failed to notice the pattern.

She soon got over her shock because Stephan was very affectionate, and made love gymnastically and with vigor, which simply took the breath from Margaret, though she was both willing and pliable. It was so amazing that soon she began to think that maybe sex was her art form. Was that possible? Maybe she could be the first sex artist? She pondered this in her mind, clearly ignorant of the porn industry's existence.

Margaret was head over heels, which left her, once again, unwilling or unable to hear advice from anyone who did not agree with her newest fantasy about her life. In less than a year, everyone she knew and loved travelled to Peconic River Farm to see Margaret, face framed in her softly regrown hair and body clad in her mother's handmade wedding dress, say "I do" to Stephan. Peconic River Farm was near the home of Stephan's parents, and they paid for the whole wedding as their gift to the couple, in order that everyone travel to them, rather than they having to go to where Margaret's parents lived. If Stephan was going to marry a weirdo, they wanted home turf.

After the wedding, Stephan insisted they move out of and away from Margaret's studio and into a respectable suburban home where a BMW looked right parked out front. It was also close enough to his very rich parents that his mother could "help" Margaret decorate, by taking her shopping and paying for the purchases. For Margaret, who had always loved to shop the most in stores hawking the well-worn and well-loved belongings of others, shopping in West Elm and Pottery Barn was definitely an uncomfortable experience. Instead of real vintage, and real wear and tear, she was now expected to buy faux or "aged" items. She was far from Callie, her parents, and even too far from the Montessori school to teach there, but Stephan had told her she should take a break from teaching to decorate their home and, perhaps, become mother to his children. Margaret's head was swimming with new fantasies. Who would she be in this world?

As in the past, Margaret's fantasies were not really grounded too much in reality. For example, she actually imagined Stephan's mother being changed by knowing her, rather than the other way around. And, as was to probably be expected, reality surprised her once again with the hard truth, and it was like a mimosa tree in the face, like a stalled out BMW on the tracks of a commuter train.

The news came as she and Stephan's mother were trying out a bed in Pottery Barn for the second guest bedroom. Stephan's mother got the call, as Stephan still had her listed as his emergency contact person in his wallet. His mother answered her phone with vinegar in her voice; she didn't like to be interrupted when explaining to Margaret again why all the guest room furniture had to match, but as soon as she heard the news she slipped off of the side of the bed and onto the floor, sobbing, her arms extended over her with the phone clasped in the hand nearest Margaret, who took the phone, said, "Hello, who is this? You've made my mother-in-law cry," and was told by a voice that her husband, Stephan, had been hit by a train because his car had stalled on the commuter rail tracks and he did not escape in time.

"Wait, so I'm a widow?" she asked. The voice said something else, and Margaret slid down to the floor next to her mother-in-law.

"I'm a widow," she said.

Stephan's mother, tears streaming down her face, turned to Margaret and slapped her hard across the mouth. "Shut up! Shut up! Shut up! You little idiot! My son is dead!"

A red print of four fingers was clearly outlined on Margaret's face. She gently reached for her mother-in-law's hand and folded it around the phone.

"It's for you," she said. With that, she rose and walked to the register. "I'm sorry to ask, but do you think you could call me a cab," she whispered to the cashier, "I've just become a widow, and I don't have a ride home."

Stephan was suddenly dead, and Margaret was back to being alone and making quick decisions without thinking them through or taking advice. That it was time to be done with Stephan's family, even his adorable niece Kennedy, Margaret could see quite clearly any time she looked in the mirror for the first week after his death. There, across her lips and cheek, were four clear fingers pointing her away from Stephan and all the trappings that had come with him, his suits, and his BMW. Stephan's mother wanted a big funeral with two days of viewings. As much as she felt her mother-in-law's hand on her face, Margaret also felt Stephan's hand on her heart, and what Margaret most wanted one last chance to have Stephan wrap himself around her on her old lumpy mattress. Mother-in-law won, as usual, and so Margaret said goodbye to Stephan's bodily form during a quiet thirty minutes the funeral director managed to eke out for her by telling Stephan's mother that they had to adjust something in the casket. Stephan looked remarkably as he had done when living, which surprised Margaret, considering the train and all. The funeral director explained that the train had actually sort of shot the Beamer off of the tracks like a rocket, and that Stephan's demise was not the result of being mowed down by the train, but the impact of being in a motionless car that was suddenly rocketed twenty feet into the woods. The motion was so sharp that it had simply whiplashed and broken Stephan's neck. His neck was covered in a silk cravat his mother had chosen, and his face looked, well, pretty good actually.

Margaret longed to touch him in the worst way, but her brain kept insisting that he was a dead thing, and she was afraid, so the funeral director let her clasp and kiss one of his own hands as she spoke to Stephan's body.

"I'm so sorry, dear Stephan, that we didn't get around to having little Kennedys of our own, and I shall really miss the amazing sex and the lovely way you always held me when we slept." She sighed so forlornly that the funeral director, who was appropriately tall, boney, and Lurch-like, did his best to fold around her and give her a good squeeze, and then he helped her make a quiet exit out the back, and put her into a nice black sedan, and had one of his underlings drive her home.

On the day after the funeral, Margaret's real estate agent held an open house for her. By Monday morning there were four good offers, one of which was a thirty-day all-cash deal. Margaret took the offer. When she was home, while waiting for the thirty days to expire, Margaret tried to look like she was out, with the curtains drawn tight. She had the locks changed, so that no one from Stephan's family could come inside and attempt to "manage" her. As for the contents of the house, Margaret used some of Stephan's money to rent a U-Haul and hired a few sturdy men from Craigslist. Within days of the open house she was dropping off Stephan's suits, and all the furniture her mother-in-law had purchased, in small batches at the closest homeless shelter she could find. She thought the patrons might really enjoy a Pottery Barn guest bed and a This End Up dining room table.

She was correct on both counts, and this gave her a renewed belief in her old decisiveness.

Margaret's parents urged her to move back home, but that did not feel like the widowey thing to do, so she turned them down. As she was packing up her personal belongings, Margaret came across the one painting she had made that she had kept (the aforementioned *Dawn Over Echo Pond*, which looked as if it should have been named *Egg-Over-Easy-ish*), and wondered if there was actually a place called Echo Pond anywhere in the world. So one day she snuck out the back door of her own house, hopped the fence, and stole through the neighbor's backyard out to the sidewalk, and down three blocks to the local library. The librarian on the desk was very sweet, and very good with her computer, and, yes, it turned out there was an actual Echo Pond. It was a real pond, just a bit off to the side of a real town, and it was due-north, true north, very very very far north. "I'd bet that lake is already frozen over by now," said the helpful librarian.

"Ha!" said Margaret, somewhat loud and forcefully for a library patron.

"Hush dear!" said the librarian. "It's going to be pretty darn cold there you know."

"It's okay," said Margaret. "I'm a widow for three weeks now. I'm used to the cold."

"Oh, that's good, but, well I'm so sorry."

Margaret reached over the counter and patted her hand. "It's nice of you to say that." Then she left the library and walked on down the street, away from her house.

She had thought she would not have to walk as far as she did, but, eventually, about an hour later, Margaret arrived at her local Jeep dealership. "I need a Jeep," she said to the first salesman who approached her, "with good tires on it and heated seats as I am moving very very far north." By the end of the day she was driving herself for the first time in years, in a warm but rugged jeep. She decided to make a few more stops, loading up the vehicle with flannel shirts and sheets, a whole set of heavy cast-iron cookware, and a sewing machine designed for quilting. She was going full-on rustic.

Neither her parents, Mrs. Potts, nor Callie were keen on the plan, regarding it about as good an idea as Rudolph the Red-Nosed Reindeer electing to seek out the Abominable Snowman.

"It's too far."

"It's too desolate."

"It's too cold."

"You'll freeze to death."

"You won't know anyone."

Margaret breathed in each worry like oxygen. She loved them all, but they were so dumb not to see that though painting wasn't the right vocation and teaching wasn't the right vocation, and sex artist wasn't the right vocation, she was still an artist. Maybe she would be a quilt artist. Maybe she would be a snow artist. But, by gum (she assumed the folks 'round Echo Pond would say 'By gum'), she was still an artist of some kind, and to go be cold and alone was what artists did. It was what artists had always done.

It took quite a few days to get close to Echo Pond. And then it took almost another full day of getting lost while trying to actually find the town-side of the pond, because the town was tiny, and in the woods, and the pond was quite big and fat and round, and the roads were not well marked, and the good Lord knows they had the Jeep's GPS beat. People who lived around Echo Pond would probably often talk about what "the good Lord" did or didn't know, and He certainly knew the Jeep's GPS was included for free for a reason: not up to snuff on the wooded roads 'round Echo Pond.

Once she'd gotten to the town, Margaret had to find the real estate agent, Berit Hagen, to take her to the little house she now owned, and set her up with all the numbers for the people she was going to need to call (roofer, plumber, mason, and the like) before the true winter set in. Berit turned out to be not an old lady, as her voice on the phone and her name itself had implied to Margaret. She did probably have 10 years more life under her belt than Margaret, but she was a happy and industrious person (she ran the little local IGA supermarket and did all the events for the senior center, which was located in the IGA's small lunch area). Berit had cherry cheeks, high cheekbones, and a head full of friendly and unruly brown curls. Plus she talked a lot, so Margaret, who talked not too much outside of what she said to herself in her own head, felt very chummy with her right away, and often dropped into the IGA on the pretense of needing eggs, or half-and-half, and ended up being able to eat lunch with Berit, which kept at bay some of the natural cold that comes from moving to a place where everybody knows everyone except you. Once Berit heard that Margaret had moved to Echo because of being a widow, she started including her in everything. Margaret found herself finger painting with the seniors, or making brownies for the book sales, brownies being Margaret's only reliable recipe.

One day the two of them stood looking out the window of the IGA, still sweaty from the Saturday Swing dance tea with the seniors, and the snow began to fall.

"Oh my gosh! It's snowing! It's not even winter yet, and it's snowing!"

"You bet it is," said Berit. "The good Lord knows we never make it to Christmas without a few snowfalls. How's your roof?"

"Done last week."

"Plumbing?"

"Three weeks ago, and drained and capped off the outside bibs last week. You said, 'the good Lord knows.'"

"Yes, because He sure does. Now how about your wood stove?"

"It's great, and Jimmy Larson chopped down a lot of the little trees I didn't want and cut them up and stacked the wood in the shed. It takes a little bit to light, but I just throw some Match Light in there, and it gets started after a while."

"Okay, you cannot use Match Light in your wood stove; you're lucky you're not already dead. I'ma get Jimmy to bring you two of those bags of pellet fuel right now, so you go home now and let him in."

"Oh, Match Light's no big thing. We used to use it to get campfire's going when I was a kid. "

"Do you own a grill?"

"No."

"Then you are not allowed to have any Match Light. It will give you carbon poisoning. Jimmy will bring your bag of it back to me. I do own a grill."

"I wanna hang out and have coffee. It's nice seeing the snow come down in this big window. And I can help bag groceries. You're gonna get a run on milk."

"We do not get runs on milk because we are sensible people and used to snow. Plus, milk doesn't do a damn thing for you in the snow. It doesn't melt ice, and do you ever get snowed in and think, 'Gosh, I want a big glass of milk?' No, 'cause grown people don't give a damn about milk unless it's to go in coffee. I'll get Jimmy to bring you a case of the sweetened condensed in case, and an extra thing of those Starbucks pods you like."

"Berit, shhh! The good Lord knows that I don't want anyone knowing I use pods!"

"We expect you to use pods, Margaret. You're an artist from a big city. We know you can't be bothered to perk. It's exotic. Go with it. You haven't lived here even half a year, so to us you're just a summer renter. And we know you don't have any time on Sunday mornings to manage to wake yourself up for church, so you really shouldn't say 'the good Lord' 'cause that might actually make someone upset with you."

"Ugh! Why do you all like church and getting up early?"

"Because our grandmas and our mothers raised us right. But you're from the city, and a widow. We don't mind."

"Aren't we friends? I bought my house from you, and you think of me as a renter?"

"Girl, hush. We are friends, but make it through your second winter and we'll be family, even if you are a heathen who sleeps through church. Family is better than friends. You know Uncle Norm?"

"Sure I do. I got all my furniture from the consignment shop."

"Well, he's married to Mark; and they have an adopted daughter, Kimani, and son, Malik, who are Echo's only black people."

"Wait, what? I didn't see any little black kids at the shop."

"You city folk are a lot dumber than I thought. Kimani and Malik go to school, like any other kids; they don't hang out all day in the shop."

"And Norm is your uncle, huh?"

"Norm and Mark came here from Chicago when Malik was three and opened up that shop. Mark started our Christmas house tour. Nobody is afraid of gay people or black people anymore. We owe that *to them*. And *they* have made it through eight winters. They are family. Now, get your newbie butt home, because Jimmy is going to be there soon with pellets, and to pick up that charcoal you promised me."

"Wow, you are bossier than my mother-in-law."

"Ex-mother-in-law, and no I'm not. Now get!" She put her hands on Margaret's shoulders, turned her from the window toward the door, and gave her a shove. "I'll come by tomorrow."

Margaret had defiantly bought some milk from the IGA before she left it, because you *did* need milk in the snow, otherwise there would be no hot chocolate. She had also picked up a case of wine, a few boxes of crackers, and a round of Boursin cheese, which was as gourmet as the IGA got.

Jimmy showed up about an hour later with a pallet full of wood stove fuel, which he unwrapped, brought in, and piled against the wall in the kitchen. It was still snowing, but he worked up a sweat lifting the big bags, and took off his two flannels to reveal some nice biceps, and Margaret did not want to be alone, so she offered him a glass of wine and a chance to help her with the cheese tray she'd fixed.

Jimmy was twenty-three to Margaret's thirty-one, and very quiet, being who he was and where he was from, but he was happy to drink free wine, eat free cheese, and show Margaret how to fill and light the stove properly. He was also fairly content, two bottles later, to sit next to Margaret on her consignment sofa and tell her about wanting to be a logger, like his dad. After they made it a glass in to the third bottle, he was not at all reluctant to have Margaret touch his biceps, and she was just brushing her lips up against his when there was a loud banging at her door, and someone calling out Jimmy's name.

He jumped up, and Margaret went to open the door, only to see Berit standing there, giving off steam from her very thoughts in the thickly falling snow.

"Jimmy, why aren't you back at the store with the truck yet?" She stomped into the house and into the kitchen, and threw a Starbucks pod into the machine like she owned the place. She pulled a travel mug from her coat pocket, filled it up with the hot coffee, and handed it to Jimmy.

"Get yourself in the truck, passenger seat, and drink this damn black coffee." She didn't have to tell the very red Jimmy twice.

"Berit-"

"Damn-it Margaret, shut up!"

"Huh?"

"Look, girly, you came here to repair yourself, and you talk about being family, well then you cannot go messing around with a young boy."

"He's not a boy!"

"Not in the city, maybe, but in Echo he's still a kid. Got it? *Got it?*"

Margaret fell back into the sofa and crumpled up. "Berit, I'm a widow, and I'm not even old. And I'm not even sad. Or happy. Or anything. I don't know what I'm going to do with myself."

"Listen Margaret, have you grieved yet?"

"What's to grieve? I'm not even sure why I was married in the first place."

"Alright, well, that's okay. You'll figure it out. And I'll come by tomorrow and plow your drive and hang out. I can't leave Jimmy just freeze in that truck, though I do want to do that for certain. Idiot boy! You're gonna be okay. Get yourself under that afghan there, and sleep it off. And I'll take that damn bag of Match Light and see you tomorrow for breakfast."

Margaret slept it off, and settled down. Berit got her into sewing by teaching her the little bit she knew, and Norm and Mark from the consignment shop hunted down fun old tea towels for her to create with. Before long, she was making little vignettes in fabric, and they actually did not look like food unless they were supposed to, so that was okay. Once again, Jimmy was back to being silent, but he kindly supplied Margaret with branches to frame the art with, and Norm hung them in the store, and Berit hung a few at the IGA, and people started buying them to hang in their houses, and not just in their kitchens.

Margaret's parents traveled all the way north to spend Christmas with her, and as much as they liked her new friends and her little house so much better than all that had come before, they were concerned by the sheer amount of snow everywhere. But Margaret told them her current plan was to keep quilting and become "family" no matter how much snow there was, so they left her with kisses and good wishes and headed back home.

Around the end of February, Berit introduced Margaret to Dr. Peter Knudsen, who came to the senior center to check out the seniors' pets, and brought along his dog, Troffel, to be petted by everyone. Troffel was a chocolate lab, and as sweet as could be. She loved everyone and everyone loved her. Dr. Peter was forty-four and a divorcee. He had met his wife in college, but she never quite adjusted to the northern life around Echo Pond, so she hadn't stayed long enough to become family. He and Margaret hit it off at once. It turned out that they both loved Troffel, and Starbucks coffee pods over perked coffee, and, stupid coincidence of all time, they both loved playing Mancala!

Soon enough, Dr. Peter and Troffel were stopping by Margaret's on snowy evenings to eat Boursin cheese and chili and play Mancala together, or Parcheesi if Norm and Mark or Berit joined them. And, as things started heating up between the two of them, the snow started melting. Little crocus buds even began to bloom in the curb grass at the IGA. And then, one night, when Margaret was just sure spring was in the air, and Berit had finally gotten in some real brie at the IGA, Dr. Peter showed up at her house with his lab, Troffel, and Luna, a little white goat with a big pink bow around her neck.

"What?"

"For you. I thought Troffel could use a friend to play with when she came over here, and then you won't be alone in the woods anymore."

As Troffel pushed past her to get her favorite chew toy that she had left on the sofa from the day before, Margaret stared at Peter, and the squirming little creature in his arms that was trying to eat his tie. Tears welled-up in Margaret's eyes.

"Get-out!" she screamed. Troffel ran over and barked at her.

"What?" Peter looked at her in confusion.

"Get out, get out, get out, and take them with you!"

Peter, Troffel, and Luna bid a hasty retreat, right to the IGA to see Berit.

"Wait," Berit told Peter. "Just wait, and hold onto the goat."

The next day the temperature dropped. Berit had thought she would hear from Margaret, but she didn't. The day after that the snow came back down. No word from Margaret. The third day at noon, Berit used her key and walked in on a sleeping Margaret, cuddled in a heap on the sofa. She made two mugs of coffee from pods and shook Margaret awake.

"Oh, hi Berit. I'm sorry; I'm not feeling well. Can you go home?" It was clear she had been crying. Even now, tears were trying to migrate over the side of her sleepy lids.

"Nope. I can't go home."

"What? Why not?"

"Havin' the place fumigated. Got hibernation beetles. Thought I'd stay with you for a while."

Margaret burst into tears. "You can't stay with me; you can't! What are hibernation beetles? Are they catching?"

"Hey," Berit sat down next to her and put her arm around her, "they're not a real thing. I was just kidding. What's wrong?"

"I don't know!" Margaret sobbed into her hands. "It's just, the weather was getting nice, and I didn't want it to get nice, and Peter showed up with a goat, and I didn't want him to show up with a goat, and Norm asked me for six more quilt pieces for the shop, and I only have five, and I don't want to do anything. I just want it to snow and snow, and never stop."

"Oh, Blackberry Winter," said Berit.

"What?"

"That's what we're having right now, got warm for a week or so, and snapped back colder and meaner than ever."

"I don't understand."

"You will when the summer comes. You got blackberry vines all over your back fence. Without this extra cold snap they wouldn't get nice and sweet like we like 'em."

Margaret sobbed into her hands again. "I don't care about the damn berries. It's the goat I'm worried about."

"You will care. Goats like berries, and I think you like that old goat."

"It's just a baby goat!" wailed Margaret, "And what do you know about it anyway?"

"I don't mean the animal, I mean the man. Peter."

"Oh my God, I cannot think about Peter!"

"Of course you can't, Margie. You haven't grieved yet. You haven't grieved that you aren't a painter, and you haven't grieved that you aren't an art teacher, and that Callie moved to Spain, and that Stephan is dead. You haven't grieved any of it."

"But I never felt like crying before until I saw that damn goat."

"Peter or the animal this time?"

"Peter. He was there, in the doorway, with his cute little baby in is arms, and oh, Berit, I think I love Peter."

"Of course you do. He suits you. But you gotta get sweet first so you can suit him."

"What happened to Luna?"

"Who?"

"The baby goat!" Margaret burst into tears again.

"Peter kept her. He's gonna keep her, and himself too I'll bet, 'till you're ready for him."

Margaret slumped against Berit's chest, cuddled into her. "What do I do now?"

"You stay hunkered down, and you think about all your past and all your losses, and you cry it out until you just can't cry anymore, and then, when you feel less cold and mean, you let that goat c'mon back in the house."

"Berit, you are the best friend I ever had. I'm never leaving Echo. I want to be family. Will you make me a grilled cheese?"

"Sure I will."

As had been the way her whole life, other people knew more about Margaret than she knew about herself. That second winter blast came on Echo hard, and Margaret never left her house. Berit brought her books to read, and movies on DVD, like *Love Story* and *The Way We Were*. Sometimes Norm and Mark came over with other Streisand movies, and they popped popcorn and cried together while the kids played Battleship in the kitchen and laughed at them. Sometimes Peter drove by and looked at the lights in her windows and cried too.

Then one day Margaret opened her back door to go to the shed for some wood, and noticed, for the first time, the vines running all along the back fence. They were starting to sprout leaves, and the snow was getting wet and melty. She didn't feel heavy anymore, or so very tired.

A few days later, most of the snow had melted, and when Margaret opened her back door, she saw a little goat eating the leaves off the vines. "Hey you, cut that out!" She went over and picked up the little goat. It tried to eat her necklace. She carried it around to the front of her house just as Troffel came bounding through the mud. There, leaning up against his truck, was Peter.

"Hey you," she said.

"Hey yourself. You like the goat after all?"

"What? Yes."

"You want it?"

"Yes."

"You want to invite it in and give it a cup of coffee and some cheese and crackers?"

"Wait, which goat are you talking about?" Margaret asked, still holding Luna in her arms.

"Both of us."

"Oh, okay. Well, do the goats wanna come in?"

"Yes they do. They miss you."

"Okay, I miss you too." Tears started down Margaret's face, and Peter was there in an instant with his arms around her, goat and all.

He kissed and smoothed her hair. "Let's go inside, and I'll make you some breakfast while you put away anything Luna might eat, which is everything. I've got a jar of Hopkin's jam that I just bought in my pocket.

"Really? What kind?

"Blackberry."

Margaret looked up at him, "Oh, I want that so bad," she said.

They turned and walked to her backyard and made their way to the open back door.

"Troffel!" Peter called and whistled sharply, and the lab was there to go inside with them. Margaret put the little goat down in front of the warm wood stove and turned and swung the kitchen door shut.

Ouch Couch

Imagine a couch
carved in ice outside the house
melting to get in.

Snow Day

The child turns and smiles
Sight of snow on landscape
Frozen fun awaits.

ON GEORGIAN BAY

William F. Crandell

TIMING IS EVERYTHING IN AN AMBUSH. You walk by a place every day and nothing happens. Then just this once it's a killing zone, and what matters is not who set it up but how awake you are. Not all ambushes involve guns.

Webb and Inga Kelly had traded cat duty with Dave Barlow and his wife dozens of times. So Dave called Webb first when he and Mary Ann planned a Thanksgiving weekend in Chicago with her family and needed somebody to feed their cats. Nobody meant anybody any harm.

"I can take Saturday, Dave," he pledged, "but Inga and I'll be gone all day Sunday. We'll be driving through the fall colors in Vermont. Okay?" Dave said it was, and he let Mary Ann know. She lined up Kimberly, the music teacher where Mary Ann taught, to fill the gap. That was that.

The trick with ambushes is the appearance of innocence. It can be useful in a marriage, too.

Webb Kelly and Dave Barlow had been friends in Basic Training. Two chess players from Ohio were bound to be swept together at a cracker factory like Fort Polk, Louisiana, in 1966. Webb was still *W.E.B.* duBois Kelly back then, a second-generation civil rights activist who called himself a Negro and joked that any army sergeant who bothered to say *nigra* rather than *nigger* was a secret liberal. Dave was a college-town white kid who grew up reading adventure novels, and having a friend like Webb Kelly was all the adventure a draftee could handle. Short of war.

It was Webb's off-balance gotta-try drive that split them up after Basic, Webb to become a stealthy Long-Range Recon Patrol commando or "LURP," and Dave to find a slot in a run-of-the-mill infantry company carrying a machinegun. The white boy from Ohio spent a year wading through the brown-green waters of the rice paddies with thirty or forty pounds of M-60 and belt ammunition, dreaming of being a LURP like his pen pal and hopping off helicopters in the dark with three or four other sneaky petes like Webb, weighed down by nothing but a rifle, greasepaint, and the certain knowledge of being outnumbered.

Ten years later, Dave Barlow ran into Webb Kelly in a bar in Columbus, Ohio. Webb was already the upside of affirmative action, a bright and hard-working state budget examiner who had just finished a Masters of Public Administration at the Kennedy School at Harvard. Married, two daughters with a son in between. Comfortable old house in an affluent north-side neighborhood. Fire-red Porsche, special order. A credit to his budget director. There wasn't enough institutional racism in America to keep Webb Kelly from going to the top, what with his talents, charm, good looks, and gears locked in overdrive.

Dave, conversely, was a coffee-ravaged reporter covering the state capitol for the Toledo paper, his career a parade of Styrofoam cups that had finally earned him the right to have his name appear on his work. His first wife had just taken back *her* name and the house. He and Webb resumed their friendship without missing a step, neither of them guessing how the train of years would take Webb Kelly for a ride.

Your life goes by like time in Vietnam: the days last forever and the months zip by like bullets. A couple of years passed, the Governor made Webb Kelly his tax commissioner in time for Webb to be asked to speak at his older daughter's college graduation. The marriage to a sharp-witted Howard grad he met at Harvard and their three kids had long since gone to the elephants' graveyard, a casualty of his first wife's self-awareness and Webb's workaholic life. After a rocky period, he had recouped brilliantly by marrying Inga Falkenhayn, the governor's stunning press secretary, who delighted in shattering images about the irreconcilability of blondes and brains, of black and white, and of feminism and happily ever-after.

The week Webb agreed to his day on cat patrol was a month before the one in which Inga Falkenhayn-Kelly gave birth to a baby it had taken four years to conceive. The seventies were over. It was 1989. You didn't need to be an astrologer to see that late in your wife's pregnancy wasn't an auspicious time to begin an affair.

"Mary Ann! We'll miss our flight!"

"Okay, okay," Dave's wife said as she shut the front door and slid into the car. "I just had to leave notes for Webb and Kimberly–our Cat Patrol."

They were halfway down the block before she finished explaining. The notes not only confirmed Impatience and Imprudence's one-can-of-tuna-a-day-apiece habit, but mentioned the other critical items on the kitchen counter: the red casserole dish that was going back to the Kellys' clean after Dave's birthday party, and the pair of undies borrowed from Kimberly when Mary Ann's period came early during a three-day teachers' retreat.

Pregnancy is the last watch before dawn that seems never to end, no matter which parent you are. Lonely and peevish, wishing he'd worn a winter coat, Webb Kelly triggered his personal ambush by using his key to the Barlows' that cold Saturday morning and stepping inside their kitchen door. He scooped up Imprudence, the marmalade tiger, and stroked his hungry belly.

"How're you doin', pal?" Webb whispered, setting the cat on the counter and opening a can of tuna.

He saw the note with his name on it and the message on the plastic bag next to Inga's casserole. "Kimberly," Mary Ann's neat writing said, "thanks for loaning me these, and for helping with the cats. Please give...." A border of black lace tugged Webb's eye away from the instructions. With the safe curiosity of a man alone in a deserted kitchen, he peeked at the panties that were waiting for—oh, sure, Kimberly *Hill*. Webb had met her once or twice at the Barlows' parties.

Kimberly (never *Kim*) Hill. Elegant, classy, sexy. Webb remembered her as the daughter of a Korean-born schoolteacher and an American lieutenant who had served in the Forgotten War. Magnificent at forty, Kimberly was a concerto for black and gold, her long straight hair a silken curtain tied back to reveal a face from an adventure film above the honey smoothness of a gymnast's body.

That was when Webb Kelly, who was anything but a mystic, had a vision. It stuck with him the next few days and nights, this image of Kimberly Hill wearing just those black lace panties. Pregnancy is the longest season, and winter was elbowing it aside. He looked up her phone number.

A month later, on a frigid mid-December night, the Barlows sat in a cream-colored waiting room with Webb Kelly outside the maternity ward at Riverside Methodist Hospital amid choking ashtrays and frazzled heaps of magazines, male decor at its most oblivious. When Mary Ann slipped into the ladies room, Dave asked his friend a question. "What's going on with you and Kimberly Hill?"

The fraying seams of the black man's eyes flinched. "Why in the world would you think I'm involved with Kimberly?"

"Why in the world would *you* think *I'm* blind?" Dave shot back. "Or stupid?"

"What can I possibly say, Dave?" Mary Ann Barlow asked three days before Christmas, her pale green eyes wide and wet. "Inga's home with her new baby, after all they went through, and she tells me yesterday that she suspects Webb is screwing around, and would I let her know if I hear anything? Then today *Kimberly* asks me to go to lunch with her and says Webb just dumped her."

"Oh?" That was all he said.

"Yeah. I had no idea there was anything between them, so I asked her about it. She said he drove his Porsche by her apartment one evening last month and asked her to go for a ride, said he'd been thinking about her, couldn't get her out of his mind."

He *is* out of his mind, Dave thought, sorting through his peas blindly with his fork. If there's one subject no married man wants his wife worrying about, it's Husbands Who Stray. Not one of Dave's faults, but . . .

". . . hungry," he heard Mary Ann say.

"Excuse me, babe?"

She frowned. "What I said was I knew Kimberly was *hungry*. She's been alone for a couple of years. I can't understand why. She's so beautiful, she's bright, she's . . ."

"All that, yeah," her husband put in, "but she's so booby-trapped. Any man with his eyes open can't miss it."

Mary Ann poured him a second glass of Merlot. Not, he hoped, to loosen his tongue. "Really?" she asked.

"Despite everything she's got going for her," the reporter said, being very careful where he stepped, "Kimberly's still looking for a perfect man to take over her life and run it to the exacting demands of a Korean-American Princess. No guy will ever be good enough. You can see it when she meets one, she's cataloging his flaws from the start. Even a bachelor'd be a sucker to walk into an ambush like that."

His wife nodded. "Is *Webb* a sucker?"

Boy, was he! Dave remembered Webb telling him, maybe five years earlier, that Asian women would always be a mystery to men who served in Vietnam. The truth, had Webb been as conscious of himself as he was readable to his close friends, was that *all* women were enigmas to him, but less than he was to himself. Webb Kelly's liability was that he took himself at face value.

The early December morning after his new daughter was born, Webb had taken Kimberly Hill to lunch and told her it was over. "People suspect," he whispered. "I don't want to hurt Inga and the baby."

It was too late for that, and had been since the first evening he dropped by Kimberly Hill's apartment under the cover of his heavy workload.

At 36, Inga Falkenhayn-Kelly was a quiet lagoon whose silver surface reflected her tranquility. It took only the first ripple of un-truth to break the mirror. She didn't have a suspicious mind, but she was in love with an honest man. They're not the best liars.

So when she asked him what was going on, and he said "Nothing," that struck her as too straightforward an answer for such a vague question. She got more specific. Webb didn't want to lie and he didn't want to hurt her, so he waffled.

Big mistake.

She got complete confirmation out of him in fifteen minutes. It didn't make either of them feel any better.

"Dave, I don't *know* why I did it," the tax commissioner told the reporter over lunch in a crowded bar. It was the day after his confession, and he was still red-eyed from moving to a motel room late the night before. Her idea.

"I love Inga, I really do," he told Dave Barlow. "This is my second marriage and I've never cheated before. I get a lot of approaches, you've seen a few, from some over-heated women I'd have chased up one hill and down another in my single days. But this time . . ."

This time, Webb Kelly said, he had followed a flight of fancy until it became a smoldering obsession. For no other reason he was aware of, he crossed over a boundary he never meant to violate, hurt somebody he'd have given blood not to hurt.

"Has a distant, familiar ring," Dave stuck in, "doesn't it?"

Webb Kelly's face was a question mark.

"I mean that good LURP stuff, those over-the-edge raids and all that."

"Bullshit."

Dave Barlow held his ground. "Then *you* explain it, buddy," he said in a flat voice. "Humans are the only animals that mate when they don't need to. You didn't screw her for love or to be a bastard, it sure as shit wasn't to get her pregnant, and you say it wasn't horniness either. What's that leave?"

His friend stared into an empty coffee mug.

"Danger and anger," Dave answered himself. "Either or both."

Dawn came, all in shades of pewter. The view of the half-empty parking lot from his second story window at the Holiday Inn didn't get any better with an inch of snow, Webb Kelly noted. Come to think of it, seeing snow flurries land on seven Japanese cars and a Chevy van wasn't worth sitting up all night for.

How long had it been since he'd seen daybreak, he wondered.

Even in summer he popped out of bed in the dark and hefted weights before downing an English muffin with low-fat margarine and a cup of black coffee as he planned his day's workload. But when had he last seen the dawn?

Webb recalled a ridgeline in the central highlands where the sun came up as a fistful of fire, far down to the east. Sergeant Kelly and one of his men—all that remained of a five-man patrol—had spent half of the longest night of their lives hidden in a clump of brush, binding their wounds in dead silence and waiting for enough light to call in so many airstrikes that a helicopter could dash in and snatch them out of a trap.

As he had outwaited the night's clammy grip, feeling now and again the unrelenting dampness of the bandages on his right hand and his thigh, Webb Kelly had counted—on four fingers—how many of the three-hundred thirty-six dawns since he got to Vietnam he'd slept through.

When it came, that sunrise outshone his imagining. "You wait, Shark Man," he told his last teammate on the chopper out, "I'll never watch another dawn again once I'm out of the army. I don't need them anymore. Nobody does. They're just sunsets on the wrong side of the sky."

Now, alone at daybreak in his motel room since Christmas, with his wife and newborn daughter Sarabeth on the far edge of his sky, in the suburbs east of the capital, Webb Kelly could tally up how much more than sunrises he had wasted by burying himself in work for twenty years, by burying himself in Kimberly Hill for twenty nights.

Funny, he mused, stubbing out the last survivor of the first pack of cigarettes he'd bought in those twenty years, funny how it doesn't even occur to me to see if Kimberly still wants me. Funny how clearly I know what I really want.

Inga almost refused to go when Webb stopped by their house to describe his bright idea. Still furious. Still raw with pain. Still numbed by relying on her head because her heart was broken.

Nobody ever told *this* woman she was cute when she was angry.

"You're sure you want *me* to go away with you," she taunted, "to Canada three days past Christmas? Is your girlfriend off wrecking another marriage? Besides, I can't leave Sarabeth three weeks after she was born. And who'll take care of our cat?"

"I don't *want* to leave the baby behind," Webb said quietly, flicking his gaze back from the silent snow, glad to see the gray sky breaking. "Dave and Mary Ann will feed Pesky."

There is no pain like betrayal, and Inga's was augmented by having had a dozen friends—some of them blacks and all of them liberals—tell her any white woman in an interracial marriage had to expect this sort of thing, whether she accepted it or not. Inga did not.

"You're crazy," the ivory-colored Valkyrie complained. "We can't afford it."

She hadn't said no yet, the reasoning part of his brain told the rest of it.

He let a little chuckle come out. "Ing, there aren't fifty families in Columbus who can afford a week at a private cottage on Georgian Bay to save their marriage as well as we can. Please?"

Inga Falkenhayn-Kelly preferred licking her wounds to binding them, and she hurt too much to say yes or no. If she was going to end up divorcing him, she said, it would be stupid of her to let him squander a dime from their joint checking or savings accounts on a futile gesture when there was little Sarabeth's future college education to think of. She glanced over his shivering shoulder toward the driveway at the only thing worth money that was totally his. Inga wanted the affair to hurt him.

Webb sold the red Porsche that weekend. They could take her car. Inga had winter blood, and she'd dragged him up north for the past few years to go cross-country skiing. He'd always gone gamely, though he told Dave Barlow that his wife's sport was simply "freezing with boards on your feet." By Tuesday, they'd be stomping snow with booted toes on a white beach along Canada's Georgian Bay on Lake Huron.

Inga hadn't said anything that didn't refer to the trip itself during the six-hour trip in her black Saab. She let Webb drive while she gave Sarabeth a bottle, angry with the universe because she produced no milk of her own. She looked out the right window without seeing a thing.

Webb gave up on trying to start a conversation after a couple of failed beginnings—one about a white-dappled orchard while they were still driving through northwest Ohio, the other about the signs in Ontario posting the speed limit in kilometers per hour. For the most part, he kept his eyes on the road and prepped for the coming debate.

It loomed over him like an approaching blizzard, like a grey and sulking sky ready to burst upon his head whenever it wanted to. All the way up to Canada, he searched for defenses, but there wasn't one that wouldn't make things worse. Just after crossing the border, he toyed with going on the attack, making it somehow *her* fault that he acted out his daydream, but he couldn't find a thing to blame her for that carried any real conviction.

Inga refused to engage, or even look at him. It was colder inside the car than outside. By the time they reached the cabin, Webb had no doubt he'd lose her. A chess player knows when to resign the game.

Certain he'd lost even before they got out of the car provided him a relief. He had nothing at stake anymore. Nothing to accomplish beside this glacial bay but an agreement on parting ways.

They walked together, not touching, on a narrow strip of beach between the cold, glittering water and the shivering pines, beside massive scarred rocks that an uncaring glacier had broken a million years ago.

The winter sun was brilliant, but it gave Webb no warmth. Nor, indeed, did Inga, her pale flaxen hair falling exactly to the shoulders of her cream-and-baby-blue Icelandic sweater, her white hands cradling the toffee-colored baby that slept in a stone-washed denim snugly against her mother's chest.

She could keep the house, he told her, and set up whatever custody arrangements for Sarabeth she wanted. They agreed that an amicable divorce would be best. No raised voices. No lawyers with feeding frenzy. No unnecessary pain. No embarrassment to the governor.

They scuffed back to the cabin in the failing light.

While Inga changed and fed the baby and crooned her to sleep in the bedroom, Webb built a fire. Then he brewed a pot of French roast decaf.

The cabin was sixty or seventy years old, its varnished knotty pine walls covered by shelves full of outdated unread novels about polite murders and bygone heroes and elegant romances that never happened. The fire and the green-shaded reading lamp cast a greeting card glow upon the living room.

"She's asleep," Inga whispered, as she picked up a mug of coffee.

They spoke for a while in soft voices about old lodges, old books, old dreams, leaving the present alone. There were long silences in which one of them would stick a log on the fire and jostle it into place with a little wrought iron poker, or pour another cup of decaf, or sample a yellowing romance novel. Once Webb looked in on his sleeping baby when he fancied she coughed, but he made no comment, gave no clue of what, if anything, he felt. He was surprised to find Inga watching him with her eyes wet.

"Do you love her that much?" she asked him.

"She's my daughter," he answered simply.

Inga hadn't asked about their child, and Webb's reply was so far from what she meant that it took her a moment to puzzle it out. Then she was annoyed. "Not Sarabeth, damn it. *Her.*"

It was Webb's turn to be dense. "Who?" he asked.

"I'm *not* going to say her name." The blazing glint in her ice-blue eyes was fire, not its reflection.

"You mean Kimber—"

"*Don't* say her name!"

"I can't believe it," he marveled, "You think I love Kimberly Hill!"

A decaying romance novel *thwacked* against the knotty pine beside his head, a late but effective wake-up call. He scooped it up in his long fingers and stood up. "Kimberly Hill," he said, "means less to me than this book." And he tossed it into the fire without a glance at it.

"Is that supposed to make me feel better?" she asked. She grabbed her down parka, jammed her feet into boots, stormed out into the peaceful night and marched angrily along the frozen lake under a haze-haloed moon, refusing its beauty and pounding the powdery snow until the chill consumed her rage.

When she slipped back into the cabin, Inga found Webb sitting cross-legged on the stone hearth, jabbing at what was left of his fire. Licks of dying flame betrayed the tear tracks on his dark face. Inga sat next to Webb and almost reached for him, but let go of the impulse and simply looked at him.

"What did you mean," he finally asked her, "do I love K . . . do I love her that much?" The rawness of his whisper confused her.

"I . . . I thought," she began, "that you brought me here, us here, to see if we could *save* our marriage, but all you've talked about is wanting a divorce. I–"

"*I* don't want a divorce," he rasped. "I thought *you* did."

"I'm here," she said in a voice she hadn't used since childhood. "I'm here."

Don't go to a peace conference with nothing to give, with no room to budge from the rightness of the positions that led you to war.

When the talks began in earnest, Webb finally spoke through the broken shell of his heart. Without blaming, without defending, he spoke his truth and heard it for the first time just as Inga did.

Danger or anger, Dave had asked him, and he finally knew which it was. It wasn't danger.

He felt so guilty when his first marriage broke up, he admitted, that he never realized how *angry* he was–angry at his first wife for leaving him, angry at himself for losing her, angry as hell that his older kids wanted a perfect father and didn't recognize that he was a real one.

With just the earliest glimmer now that it had been a rationalization, Webb Kelly remembered deciding that a trained killer who had traded his tiger camouflage for a three-piece suit couldn't afford to get angry. His chess-player's rationality and his middle-class Black cautiousness had buried his anger where he thought it would do no harm.

Deep inside.

Then, without warning, he had stumbled into a richer love than the first marriage he had let die untended. Inga was as dazzling to talk to as to stare at, and the unleashing of their passion had been the great surprise of a romance between two careful, correct careerists who couldn't wait to touch each other's skin.

When they had planned their lives together, the easiest agreement was that having children wasn't a high priority. Webb's kids were teenagers in New Jersey, and their infrequent visits were never very satisfying. Besides, there was no way Inga's ambition could be stalled by babies.

A year into a happy marriage, though, and with the governor

safely reelected, Inga had listened not to her body's ticking but to her own open heart. A baby became a priority. Webb, who would do anything rather than blow this perfect marriage, said not a word about how much he dreaded going through fatherhood again–about how angry he felt at Inga for changing the contract. Not a word to Inga, not a word to himself.

The baby didn't come easily. During the first year they listened while friends and family coached them to relax. A year is *nothing*, everybody said. Then came year two, full of simple solutions: the yeast infection that needed patience, the sperm count that had to be taken three times because a lab technician dropped a decimal point, the minor surgery to open Inga's blocked tubes. During year three she waited month after month amid pregnant women and fussy babies in a popular doctor's crowded reception room so she could be injected with a drug that worked in most cases. But not for her.

Webb kept quiet, secretly relieved, wishing she'd give up.

In year four, with Webb's anger hidden so deep beneath *her* longing that he lost all sight of it, he learned to give her twice-daily injections of a medicine they couldn't have paid for without their state employee coverage: little glass vials of fluid donated by menopausal women in Europe that a pock-marked young specialist thought might jump-start Inga's ovaries.

Which they finally did.

Once, in Vietnam, Webb Kelly had tossed a bunch of faulty ammunition into an abandoned well in a ruined village his team had used as a base for three days. When it was time to leave, he decided that there was some danger that the local guerrillas would go down after it and use it in booby traps, even though the Americans had turned the hole into a latrine. Webb dropped a hand grenade into the depths to destroy the bullets and they all exploded at once, as he always told the tale, "blowing the crap out of Vietnam."

The booby trap of his mature years got its explosive charge from his buried anger about the baby he never wanted. The black lace undies and the elegant, hungry music teacher simply provided the tripwire.

If you're a man talking with your wife about your own infidelity, you might think you've already opened the most dangerous can of snakes. You *might* think that, unless she's just had a baby you tell her you wish hadn't been born.

An hour after that, exhausted from screaming and crying, Inga went to the bedroom overlooking Georgian Bay alone, without once letting Webb touch her. She slept the sleep of the just for the first time since having her baby, and awoke in fear to see the sun well above the trees and the crib empty. "*Sarabeth!*" she gasped as she sprang to the bedroom door.

In the center of a pool of lemon light, a handsome Black man sat cross-legged on the floor with a baby girl on his lap, both of them making pigeon sounds. Outside a picture window, diamonds danced on Georgian Bay. Once Inga's heart stopped racing, it melted.

"I, um, Sarabeth's being so *good* for not having her bottle yet," she said softly, barefoot in her white flannel nightgown.

Her husband–he hadn't stopped being that–grinned. "Babe," he said, "you were a high school cheerleader when I fed my *first* daughter so my wife could sleep. I came and fed Sarabeth before daylight so she wouldn't wake you."

"Did *you* sleep?"

"Not much," he admitted. "Central heating notwithstanding, I kept watch over the fire most of the night."

Inga sat beside him on the shearling rug and said nothing. Tears formed at the edges of her eyes and rolled with majestic slowness down the pale slopes of her face.

"I've never seen you with a baby," she told him. "That first week, before we fought–you didn't really want Sarabeth, did you?"

Webb shook his head ever so slightly, as if there was a chance that his daughter understood spoken English. "*You* wanted her so much I just let you mother her."

"The perfect mother," she mocked. "The perfect press secretary becomes the perfect mother and the perfect ex-wife."

It was quiet in the cabin for an unbearably long time, perhaps twenty seconds.

"I'd like you to fail at the last of those," Webb said.

And she did. While sleep had darned the tattered edges of her heart, her husband had fallen in love with her daughter–*his* daughter. Their daughter.

"I really hadn't thought much," Inga admitted, "about you as a father. Or whether it was fair to demand that you raise a second generation of kids."

"Thank God for that," he laughed, "or I'd never have had this second chance."

Outside, winter went on without them. They stayed in the cottage on Georgian Bay for the rest of the week, and then for one more. They warmed each other's skin, each other's heart. They played with their baby. They let time have its way with them. They fell in love again and rewrote the rules.

"Do we need to make sure Dave and Mary Ann are feeding Pesky?" Inga remembered to ask one morning.

Her husband just laughed. "The deal I cut was they'd do it till I tell them not to. Dave agreed they owe us."

And once, in the second week they were there, a local police officer drove out to tell Webb that the governor of Ohio was trying to reach him by phone. "Next time he calls," Webb suggested, "tell him I left a totally competent deputy commissioner in charge. Uh, *not* totally competent, just *competent*."

That New Year, Webb and Inga gave up being perfect. They settled for being real and having some time with their baby and each other. Oddly enough, the governor respected that. Oddly enough, their friends liked them even better. Oddly enough, Webb and Inga laughed a great deal from deep inside about the ambush that saved their lives.

A COUGH AT THE COLLEGE
OF THE PACIFIC

David Yurkovich

IT WAS SNOWING IN VEGAS. I veered off East Flamingo Road and headed north on Spencer Street doing forty and, despite the fact that it weighed nearly as much as an M4 Sherman tank, the Subaru fishtailed sharply into oncoming traffic. I frantically sought to regain control, barely missing a US Mail truck, though not the subsequent obscenities issued from its driver.

Anyone who knows anything about Vegas will tell you that snow is as rare as a million-dollar casino payout. The last measureable snowfall–1.3 inches–had occurred a quarter century ago, in 1972. I down shifted and turned left onto Chippewa Drive, arriving at 1683 a minute later. My fingers kept time against the wheel as "I'll Never Smile Again," track 5 of the Dave Brubeck Quartet's *Jazz at the College of the Pacific*, radiated from the car speakers like audible velvet.

I switched off the ignition, fumbled across a snow-dusted sidewalk, and rang the doorbell of the red stucco mid-century modern, glancing at its adjacent kidney-shaped pool as flurries blew around my face.

"Maybe you're a good omen," I whispered to a dozen tiny snowflakes. "I could use some favorable news."

The front door and its faded mahogany stain creaked slowly open. An elderly woman dressed in green flannel pajamas peered at me through a small opening. Her skin was leather dry and the color of the desert sand at sunset from too many years spent in this typically hot and arid climate. She pushed a thin line of ash white hair out of her face.

"Yes?" she asked.

"I'm looking for Sara or John Tonkinson."

"I'm Sara."

"Do you mind if I come in? It's freezing out here."

"What do you want?"

"I was hoping to ask you a few questions about music, about a concert, actually. One you attended some time ago."

She performed an ad hoc visual inspection and swung open the door. "If you've come here to rob me, you're in for a disappointment, unless you specialize in purloined photos of grandchildren."

The door closed behind us. Her small frame was dwarfed by the entranceway of her home. The interior of the house was dark, as most of the curtains were tightly shut. Red and green flashing lights draped across a three-foot-high plastic Christmas tree in the corner of the living room flashed on and off.

"Can't recall the last time I saw it snow," she said. "Would you like coffee? I have Folger's and Sanka. The Sanka's better."

"No thank you."

Mrs. Tonkinson sat on a nearby recliner. "So what's this all about? You mentioned something about a concert?"

I introduced myself and began relating the tale, but paused after a minute.

"It might be easiest if I spoke with you and John together, just to keep from repeating myself or taking up too much time."

"John's dead."

"My, um, deepest condolences, Mrs. Tonkinson," I frowned. Not the first time mortality had gotten in my way. She mistook a weary expression as genuine compassion, so I pressed ahead. "When did he die?"

"Just earlier this year. Sudden myocardial infarction."

86

"I'm so sorry," I said, pausing a moment. "About the concert, perhaps you can help since you were there, too. Do you recall anything specific about that night? Anyone look sick, for instance? A cold or the flu?"

"It was a long time ago. I'm afraid I don't remember much about it, aside from the flowers."

"Flowers?"

"Yes, from John. It was our first date and he bought me flowers. Beautiful lilacs."

"And the concert?"

"We were both enrolled at College of the Pacific. It was a great time to be there. Brubeck and his band played there often. But I don't recall anyone being ill during any of the events we attended, if that's what you're asking. I was young and in love, and it's been too long."

"I understand."

"I hope you find the answers you're looking for."

"Thanks, me too," I said.

Once outside I walked toward my car. Grey skies had given way to blue and the snow had stopped. "So much for good omens," I said.

I switched on the ignition and fired up the heater. Growing up on the East Coast I'd been immune to cold weather, but after a few months in LA I found myself reliant upon coats and jackets whenever the thermometer dipped below sixty. As air from the car vent warmed my cold hands, I removed a weathered and folded sheet of paper from my wallet uncapped the pen from my shirt pocket, and updated the list.

John and Sara Jonkinson
1683 Chippewa Dr.
Las Vegas
(no phone)

Seventy-six dead ends. Three still to be determined. I refolded the paper and placed it back in my wallet and headed toward I-15 South and the five-hour drive back to Los Angeles. Once on the interstate, I switched on the Subaru's cruise control. A faux leather 75-CD holder labeled "JAZZ – A THRU C" rested on the passenger seat. I flipped past the Albert Ayler Trio's *Spiritual Unity*, Chet Baker's *Baby Breeze*, and Art Blakey's *Moanin'*, before stopping at a bootleg copy of *"azz at the College of the Pacific* by The Dave Brubeck Quartet. The bootleg version was purportedly recorded from original studio master tapes long thought lost. I'd purchased it six months earlier at the Malibu Jazz Music Convention for sixty bucks. The audio was louder, the highs and lows more pronounced. Within seconds I felt reconnected to my youth. The vibrant sleeves of the albums that comprised my parents' expansive vinyl collection, the crisp and cool New England autumn air. Memory and sensation blending seamlessly like milk into tea.

I decreased speed as the familiar, up-tempo sounds of Track 1, "All the Things You Are," fronted by Paul Desmond's flawless and improvisational alto sax playing, engulfed the interior of the wagon's custom-designed quadraphonic speakers. Dave Brubeck's piano added to the uniqueness of the tune as his solo progressed from J. S. Bach musings into a powerful and vivid climax of sound. Nine minutes and twelve seconds later the tune slowed to its inevitable end amidst overwhelming audience's applause.

Traffic was light as Track 2, the ballad "Laura," began with its slow romantic cascade of piano keystrokes that seemed to glide, harp-like, against the soft brush work of Wisconsin-born drummer Joe Dodge. Fifty-nine seconds into the track, I increased speed again, knowing too well what lingered on the musical horizon. I counted down the remaining seconds to the inevitable moment, the moment that had become my latest obsession. Exactly eighty-four seconds into the track, atop Brubeck's piano playing, Dodge's brushing, and Ron Crotty's bass, a penetrating cough erupted from the audience. A damning, careless cough, caught on tape and permanently staining an otherwise flawless, masterful recording of jazz improvisation. I skipped ahead to the next track but soon ejected the disc and drove in silence.

Darkness enveloped Los Angeles as I entered my apartment and switched on the lights. Once, not long time ago, O'Brien would have greeted me at the door amidst gentle purring. But O'Brien was gone, having escaped through an open kitchen window on a rainy October evening. I'd always assumed cats hated water, but I suppose curiosity had gotten the better of O'Brien, rain be damned. Long searches had proven unsuccessful, though I kept the window open, hoping he might one day return.

I grabbed a Sapporo from the fridge and retreated into the living room. After five minutes of news I switched off the TV and switched on the stereo receiver, hitting the CD PLAY button before falling onto the sofa. The music of *Jazz at the College of the Pacific*, files ripped from a pristine copy of the original Fantasy Records vinyl pressing of 1953 and processed through an anti-static charger, eclipsed the silence of the room. A car pulled into the driveway and moments later Lien Chen, my next-door neighbor for the past two years, peered through my living room window.

"It's unlocked, c'mon in," I said, a bit too loudly.

Lien entered, dressed, as usual, in black yoga pants and a heather gray tie-back tank.

"Hard day at the office?" I asked.

"Just the usual," she said. "Instructing rich housewives who've nothing better to do than master downward facing dog before driving two blocks to drop ninety-dollars on an Anthropologie tank top." Lien snagged a bottle of pomegranate cherry water from the fridge and took a seat next to me. We'd been neighbors for five years, having both arrived in LA during the same week. "How'd the Vegas trip go?"

"Not good. Husband, deceased; wife, no recollection."

"That sucks. Are you about ready to give up this obsession?"

"Not yet. Not quite yet."

"Figured as much, seeing as how you're playing that same damn live album yet again."

Desmond's gentle sax on "For All We Know" filled the air, and we sat in silence for a tranquil moment.

"Did you ever stop to wonder," I began, "what the world might have been like had Brubeck followed his original career path and become a veterinarian rather than switching his major to music in 1939?"

"I can't say that I have," Lien said.

"I mean, sure we'd still have Kenny Burrell, Cecil Taylor, Dexter Gordon and the like. But a world without Brubeck/Desmond collaborations? I can't even ponder it."

"Unless he used his gift of music to heal sickly animals."

"Good point," I admitted. "Hadn't considered that."

"It was a joke. You really have to pull back the reigns on this.

I mean, you've gone full OCD over a split-second cough recorded on a live album forty-five years ago. Do you really expect to find any answers?"

"That's still the plan," I said, trying to laugh off Lien's frustration.

"I don't get it," she said, head shaking.

I opened the black three-ring binder that was never too far beyond reach. "There's not much to get. Brubeck met alto saxophonist Paul Desmond in 1944 while in the US Army. After the war, in 1951 he joined Brubeck's quartet. Brubeck had already been recording on the Fantasy Records label. The last album he recorded for Fantasy was 1953's *Jazz at the College of the Pacific*. Ron Crotty on bass and Joe Dodge on drums rounded out the band."

"That's all great, but what does it have to do with anything?"

"It's all relevant, or might be. The cough on "Laura" occurs at one-minute twenty-four seconds. Eighty-four seconds. A deep cough, undeniably male."

"I know. You've played it for me before. A lot. But again, so what?"

"Used to drive my dad nuts. Got to the point where he couldn't even listen to the track."

"Like father, like son."

"Yeah. I guess I've slowly inherited his frustration about it," I admitted.

"Phone calls and in-person visits with seventy-nine people who attended Brubeck's December 14, 1953 concert. I'd say it's more than frustration."

"No one can recall hearing the cough at the time of the performance. It's baffling."

"Because it's a forty-five-year-old cough! I mean, what do you want?"

"I guess I just want to know why, Lien. Why didn't he—whoever *he* is—just get up from his seat and walk to an area away from the mics? Or couldn't he have just, ya know, held it in, borrowed a mint from his date? I just want to know; Lien. I need a bit of closure."

"Clearly. But what if it never comes?"

"Finish my film project, graduate with the rest of the Class of '99, and continue mooching off my family until I can find a job I guess."

"You're living the American dream. But just FYI, the center is hiring spin class instructors, if you're ever, you know, interested in earning money."

"I don't even want to know what that means."

"Spin class?"

"Earning money. Spin class also." I walked toward a hand-made map suspended on the living room wall.

"Lookie here. Each of these twenty-eight pushpins represents a city I've traveled to on this search." I handed Lien a half sheet of paper. "Three more leads yesterday—three! Probably the final of the lot since everyone else appears to be senile or dead."

"Maybe both, based on some of the escapades you've shared."

"At least this trio is local."

"Sure, if you consider Santa Monica to Pasadena local. Which, by the way, no one does."

"Still, could be the break I've been waiting for."

"Then why don't you just pick up the phone?"

"In person is better. Very easy to hang up on an unknown caller; less easy to shut a door in someone's face," I noted. "What's your schedule like for tomorrow?"

"Too busy to drive to Pasadena."

"C'mon, it'll be fun. You can tell all your friends you were there when I finally solved the greatest puzzle known to man."

"Or when you didn't, and plunged a dagger through your heart in despair. Sure, count me in."

The following morning Lien and I breakfasted on avocado over eggs Benedict at the Third Street Promenade where ten-foot synthetic candy canes nearly outnumbered the jacaranda trees. We determined the best route would be Thousand Oaks to Silver Lake to Pasadena, followed by a late lunch at Lawry's in Beverly Hills.

We hit the road at 10:05 AM. The North 405 volume was surprisingly moderate and the 101 West was smooth sailing until De Soto where a stalled vehicle resulted in a twenty-minute delay. Still, the trek from Santa Monica to Thousand Oaks took only forty-five minutes.

"You wanna wait here or come along?" I asked, as we approached Sunny Lane, a narrow dead end street adjacent to Santa Rosa Road.

"Maybe I'll wait here," Lien said, retrieving ear buds from her purse. "Good luck."

Harold Phineas Greenspan, who occupied the top floor of 221 Sunny Lane, an upscale senior-living housing development created in the 1970s, greeted me with blank stares. It was all downhill from there.

"I'm assuming swing and a miss?" Lien asked, glancing at my frown as I opened the car door minutes later.

"Don't ever use sports idioms with me!" I exclaimed. "But yeah, your assumption's correct. Harold's golden years are gold plated at best. His memory's largely gone. Thinks Brubeck is a game show host."

"That sucks. Maybe you'll have better luck in Silver Lake."

We sat in endless traffic on the 101 East, curiously watching as police cruisers and ambulances raced along the shoulder of the road toward an accident somewhere ahead.

"This is the problem with LA traffic," I noted as a fire rescue vehicle raced by. "It's inevitable you'll be delayed by some multi-car pile-up, but by the time you reach the point of impact, there's nothing to see."

"Too much to ask for a mangled corpse upon an embankment, I suppose," Lien said, eyes glued to the latest issue of *Self*.

"Exactly."

Cars and trucks were ushered into a single lane by members of the LAPD. Once past the delay, we continued toward the Silver Lake Boulevard exit and merged onto North Dillion. A quick left onto Marathon and we soon reached the Robert B. Anderson Center for Advanced Healthcare. Lien and I entered the reception area and I asked to see Demetria Adamson.

"Are you family?" the receptionist asked.

"Nephew," I lied.

Two forged signatures later and we were pointed toward the common area, a sad gathering place that reeked of moth balls and urine, and occupied by senior women in various stages of physical and mental decline. Long strands of silver tinsel garland, upon which hung dozens of candy canes, adorned the walls along with Christmas drawings done by random grandchildren. We asked around and soon found eight-eight-year-old Demetria seated in a green fabric recliner in the corner of the room, and provided some exposition to explain our impromptu visit.

"Of course I know Dave. Used to. Knew him fairly well," she said, adjusting the crocheted blanket atop her small frame.

"You personally knew Dave Brubeck." I said.

"We were both music majors at UP. Did you know Dave couldn't read music? Not a single note. It was quite the controversy at the time and the administration was in a quandary. How to graduate a gifted student who admittedly couldn't perform one of the basic foundations of the trade?"

"What happened?" Lien asked.

"He graduated, of course, but UP made him promise to never teach music. Isn't that silly?"

"Bureaucracy at its most bureaucratic. You attended the December 14, 1953, concert?" I asked.

"I went to every show for many years. Trio, quartet. They performed constantly, and Dave's star shone brighter and brighter. Before long I was just another face in the crowd, but that was okay." Demetria paused to sip from a plastic water bottle. "As for this cough you mentioned, I don't recall hearing it. But really, at that time and with the limited recording technology available there was always a lot of background noise showing up. Haven't you ever listened to *Brandenburg Gate* or *Newport 1958* or even *Park Avenue South*? Anyway, what's a cough really? What's it matter?"

We talked for a few moments more then said farewell.

"Whip smart, she was. I hope I'm that sharp when I'm eight-eight," Lien said, as we approached the car.

"She may be smart, but she's wrong. It does matter. Matters to me anyway."

"Let's see what awaits us in Pasadena."

Pasadena turned out to be a bust. Lynden Ellwood could neither see nor hear us. His caregiver, an uptight, monogynous personal assistant named Alejandra, explained that he'd lost both senses following a massive stroke two years earlier. She refused to let us in and promptly closed the door.

"I guess it actually *is* easy to shut a door in someone's face," I said, and dropped down onto the sidewalk in defeat.

I was feeling too depressed to drive, so Lien took the wheel. We were twenty minutes from Lowry's, heading west on Beverly Boulevard. I had no appetite but a deal was a deal.

"Look," Lien said, "you tried. Tried harder than most people try at things. Perhaps this would be a good time to wrap up your film project. Closure, you know?"

I nodded and we traveled in silence for a few minutes.

"Why are you pulling over?" I asked, as we crossed Normandie.

"When I'm upset, I shop. You try it."

"I don't wanna shop. Anyway, where would I shop? Nothing around here but restaurants and convenience stores."

Lien pointed to the left. "Just saw the sign: grand opening."

"Smokescreen Vinyl." Another shitty used record store in a city where shitty used record stores were plentiful. I sighed, knowing that Lien wasn't going to take no for an answer. "Keep it running. I'll be back in two minutes. Maybe less."

I dashed across the boulevard between moving cars. It was a tiny shop, first floor of a split-level mid-century modern in disrepair. I considered turning back, but the distant sound of John Coltrane's alto sax flowing from quad speakers mounted on the exterior walls lured me in.

Very quickly I realized that the store had been aptly named. Nothing about the exterior prepared me for the jazz and blues vinyl treasures within its four walls. Bill Evens, Wayne Shorter, Herbie Hancock, Sonny Rollins, Art Ensemble of Chicago, Oscar Peterson. I thought about the pittance of cash in my wallet and wondered if Lien might be willing to offer me a short-term loan.

Through a tedious and time-consuming process of elimination I narrowed my selections down to five albums, all gems. The shining star, a pristine copy of the 1968 Japanese reissue of *Jazz at the College of the Pacific*. Pressed on 200-gram heavyweight vinyl, it reflected one of only two albums released on the short-lived Cherry Red label. The asking price, a meager five-dollars, was staggeringly low. I approached the cash register where an older man, large frame, dark complexion, sporting a white linen shirt and khaki pants, stood reading a copy of *DownBeat*.

"This shop is amazing," I said. "I can't believe I'm your only customer."

"I'm pleased that you like it," he said, and extended a hand. "Niles Hannaford Washington. You can call me Niles. We only just opened this week. Anyway, not a lot of interest in vinyl these days, but we'll do okay with mail order. Big international customer base." He sorted through my selections, nodding in approval, then smiled.

"*Maiden Voyage*. Great recording. I was supposed to engineer this record but had other commitments at the time with Cheshire Records, so Alfred Loin handled production. I suppose he did okay." Niles chuckled to himself, an in-joke kind of laugh that was beyond my understanding.

"Are you still in the business, Niles?" I asked, feeling equal parts anxious and awkward.

"No. Not for a few years. Last studio work I did was Weather Report's *Night Passage*. Five, six years ago. You play?"

"Only records. My parents raised me on jazz."

"Good jazz or bad jazz? That is, old school or progressive?"

"Old school."

"That's good to hear. Your folks could have done a lot worse."

I didn't want to ask the question, because I was afraid of the answer. But we were already talking so I blurted it out. "You ever work with Dave Brubeck?"

"Oh, not so much, no. Teo Macero produced a lot of Dave's work. Nice guy, Teo. We called him the producer's producer." He glanced again at my selections and held up *Jazz at the College of the Pacific*. "It surprises me that someone like you, someone raised on good jazz, wouldn't already own this record."

"I own several copies, but I've never seen this pressing before."

"Excellent pressing. I actually worked on this record. Second engineer. Uncredited of course, but good money nonetheless. Sound board was a relic from the Stone Age, but you work with what you've got."

I pointed my index finger at the album cover. "You were at this show, December 14, 1953?"

"I've seen Brubeck live more times than you've gotten laid, far back as the early Blackhawk gigs. That's where he got his big break. No one was playing jazz like that nowhere. It shook up the city, I can tell ya that much. San Francisco was old school jazz until Dave came along and woke the sleepers. I remember seeing a thirteen-minute variation of 'Varsity Rag' that blew the roof off the joint. Pure magic. And yes, like I said, I assisted on the recording of this album and as such was present on the evening of the show."

"Then you know about the cough."

Niles paused. "Of course I do. We used to refer to this record as *A Cough at the College of the Pacific.* Goddam shame."

I pinched my right arm until it hurt, because I felt certain I was dreaming. "Just to be sure we're on the same page, Niles, I'm talking about an audible background cough, a slight but definite hacking sound, recorded on "Laura," track 2."

"Yeah, we're on the same page."

"Jesus. Do you know what this obsession's been like? Headaches, insomnia. Lot of insomnia. I've been trying to locate the source of that cough for months. You have no idea."

"Doesn't sound too healthy," Niles said, smiling.

"I can't fathom it. How could someone hack during a live recording?"

Niles' smile faded and he placed the album on the counter. "Boy, you don't have a fucking clue."

I stared blankly into his eyes a moment then sheepishly turned away.

"The cough you're referring to, the one that's been keeping you up at night, belongs to Hardwick Abernathy." Niles pointed at one of a dozen framed photos on the wall behind him. "That's Hardwick and me at the Chicago Jazz Festival in '51. Hardwick worked sales for Blue Note, EMI, Columbia. Knew the name of every record shop owner from San Antonio to Saskatchewan and all points east and west. He logged more air miles than the most seasoned pilot and visited more cities than a traveling circus strong man. Went to towns most black men dared not to enter. I invited him to the show that night, December 14 as you noted, but he would've come anyway. As for the audience, incidental noise was always captured during live shows. Sometimes we sweetened it out during the mix, sometimes we didn't. So I paid it no mind. Wasn't until later, when the house lights came up and the auditorium began to empty, that someone noticed Hardwick was still seated, eyes closed. Figured he'd just nodded off."

"But he hadn't?"

"Hardwick was dead before he ever reached the ER. Found out later it was a brain aneurysm what killed him. Terrible loss. Left behind a wife and two boys."

Niles pulled a pack of smokes from his shirt pocket and lit a cigarette.

"Lucky Strike?"

"Thanks, that's okay."

"Didn't feel right mixing out the cough. Now you know, you feel any better?"

"Not really, no."

"Sometimes the answer we're looking for isn't what we expect. Not what we'd like it to be."

The front door opened and Lien entered.

"Thought you got lost," she said.

"Just talking music," I said.

I paid for my purchases and nodded at Niles.

"Thanks."

"You take care now, and stop back again soon."

"I will."

Lien and I dashed across the busy street and hopped back into the car.

"I'm sorry today's been a bust," she said, as we headed west toward Lawry's. "Maybe some questions weren't meant to be answered."

"Yeah, guess so." I wanted to share my new revelation with Lien, but felt conflicted. This wasn't the outcome I'd been anticipating. The thought of telling the story to anyone seemed wrong. Perhaps one day, but not yet.

After lunch, Lien and I returned home and she was soon off to work. As darkness fell upon Santa Monica, I glanced out window and watched as a scraggy gray feline dashed along the sidewalk before vanishing in the shadows. I stepped outside, dry kibble secured in my left hand, and made silly cat noises the likes of which only cat owners can make. The stray, a skinny no-tag mess of matted fur with an obvious eye infection, approached eagerly and was scooped up without protest. As we headed back, a family dressed in t-shirts, shorts, and sandals emerged from their home. Red and green lights were quickly draped atop a myriad of ill-maintained topiary. The strands glowed as

"We Wish You a Merry Christmas" began playing on an endless loop in eight-bit sound to the delight of the kids. Once inside, I acclimated my fuzzy roommate to his home, taking care to tightly shut the kitchen window.

That night, as New O'Brien slept, I boxed up notebooks, ledgers, receipts, and other papers that had defined my life for the past year. The map and its many push pins came down. I dropped the new vinyl onto the turntable and sipped hot coffee. Eighty-four seconds into "Laura" a dead man's cough echoed through my home, as it had done on so many prior occasions. But whatever angst I'd felt previously was gone, replaced with a sense of calm and sorrow. Freedom quickly enveloped me. Freedom from anger, from bias. The track continued along at thirty-three and one-third revolutions per minute before dissolving into the up tempo crowd pleaser "Lullaby in Rhythm." I fell onto a soft chair, shut my eyes, and soon drifted into a tranquil sleep.

Christmas arrived. My landlady looked in on New O'Brien while I spent the holiday in Rhode Island with my parents. Their Park Street house felt smaller than I'd remembered, but it was still massive when compared with my small apartment.

Dad's record collection had grown, even in the short few months since my last visit. A recently installed built-in bookcase housed most of the vinyl. While sorting through his latest pearls, I decided to share the tale. Seemed only right since I'd inherited the "cough" obsession from him anyway.

"You don't find it all just a bit too convenient?" he said, after some time.

"What do you mean?"

"What I mean is, you went out looking for answers and struck out. I get that; it was a long shot anyway and, frankly, I'm surprised at your tenacity. But then, entirely by coincidence, your friend Lien just happens to drop you off in front of a used record shop that just happens to be staffed by a man who just happens to have all the answers at his fingertips. It doesn't add up."

"It does if you believe in coincidence," I countered.

"Do you?" he asked.

Following my return to Santa Monica, I sought to disprove

Dad's suspicions. But neither the Los Angeles Public Library system nor the World Wide Web of 1997 provided the answers I wanted.

On January 3, Lien, just back from a visit to Beijing, invited me to breakfast at her apartment. Over waffles and coffee we exchanged gifts as well as travel tales. We cleared the plates and I unwrapped a twelve-inch square package that was obviously vinyl.

"*Head Hunters* by Herbie Hancock," I said, eyeing the colorful front cover artwork. "Nice. This was on my to-buy list."

"I'm glad you don't already own it. The receipt's attached in case you want to exchange it for something else."

"Smokescreen Vinyl," I said, glancing at the paper invoice as my heart sank. "I didn't mention this to you before, but on that day we stopped at the record store, I got all the answers I needed from the sales clerk–from Niles."

Lien smiled. "That's terrific!"

"It was."

"What do you mean, *was?*"

"My Dad said it all sounded too good to be true. Said it was too much of a coincidence. I guess he was right."

"I still don't follow."

"See, problem is, this gift receipt here is dated one week *before* our day-long trek across town. I thought it was random, us stopping there. It wasn't though, was it?"

Lien sighed. "There are two things I know about you," she said. "One, you needed closure on this Brubeck obsession. Two, you were never, *ever*, going to get closure."

"So you gave it a nudge."

"Basically."

"And Niles, assuming that's actually his name–"

"It isn't."

"Niles didn't actually work as a sound engineer on any of Brubeck's recordings."

"No."

"Nice of him to play along though. How'd you pull this together?"

"Luck mostly. I was in the area, holiday shopping, and stumbled upon the record store. Figured I might find a decent gift for you. Niles and I–his name's Mick, not that it matters–Mick and I started talking music. He asked me what you liked. At some point, your fascination with the 'cough' became part of the conversation. I explained how it'd been gnawing at you and, well, he offered to help."

"Altruism in the city of the angels. Who'd have thought?"

"Not too altruistic. I paid him fifty bucks."

"So no one named Hardwick Abernathy died during the recording of *Jazz at the College of the Pacific*."

"Highly unlikely."

"Why then?"

"Because I'm your friend. Because you needed to get on with your life and I knew you weren't going to do it any other way."

"I suppose I should thank you."

"Probably you should."

"But I'm not going to." I sighed. This wasn't the closure I wanted. Wasn't closure at all, really. But it was something. "It's okay, really. I appreciate you looking out for me. Happy New Year."

We toasted. Tea cups in lieu of champagne.

"Happy New Year," Lien said, coughing unexpectedly as she swallowed.

"Are you okay?"

"I'm fine," she said, after a moment. "You know, sometimes a cough is just a cough."

PAW PRINTS IN THE SNOW

Bayne Northern

"HI, STAN! HI, MARCIA!" Carey called out, interrupting the couple, strolling side by side, as they walked down the street with their two dogs in tow. The couple waved.

It was 3:00 PM and Carey had been awaiting their arrival. She knew that Stan and Marcia passed by her new house in the little beach hamlet of Ocean Dunes every day at this time.

"Have you seen him today?" Carey asked. She was dressed in a purple, puffer jacket, convertible mittens, and a white, bubble beret. Her right-side coat pocket bulged with dog treats, while the left held a slightly exposed squeak toy. A leash hung around her neck. Carey was prepared for an extended search and rescue.

"Not so far today." Stan stopped and turned to face her, his kind smile barely visible under his full mustache. He wore faded Levis and a flannel shirt that was largely obscured beneath a navy, wool pea coat. His light, blue eyes shone brightly behind thin, wire-rim glasses.

"Our friend, Rob, saw him yesterday evening as the sun was

setting." Marcia said, adjusting the zipper of her grey car coat and pulling up her thick scarf wrapped tightly around her neck. "The beagle was walking down the boardwalk. Rob said the poor thing had a salt water taffy wrapper stuck to his ear."

"Rob put some food out for him," Stan added. "Dog wouldn't come close 'til he went inside."

"Carey, I'm really glad you agreed to help us rescue this stray." Marcia smiled at her.

"I do love animals, especially those that are lost or abandoned. Since moving to Ocean Dunes, I've already saved a cat and a bird with a broken wing. I hope I have the same good luck with the beagle. I've been feeding him some days. He usually shows up around mid-morning. He peeks out from under the bushes with his soulful eyes watching me put the food down. He won't take a bite until I go inside either." Carey sounded frustrated.

Stan nodded his head, understanding the cautiousness of strays. The two dogs sat down, realizing their afternoon stroll had come to a halt.

"Do you think he was abandoned? What an awful thing to do to a pet! So cruel." Carey grimaced at the thought of people deserting their pets, pulling her coat tighter as a frigid gust of wind kicked up. She reached down and gently stroked one of Stan and Marcia's rescues.

"It appears that way. Honestly, Carey, I worry about him with winter approaching. He could starve, get injured, or freeze to death." Marcia said worriedly. She then squatted down to cup her mixed lab's head in her hands and softly caress his muzzle.

"I know! It breaks my heart to see him staring at me. If I could only get close enough to capture him."

Marcia looked up at Carey with a thoughtful expression. "Stan and I were discussing the stray with Rob and the Petersons. We think we should stop feeding him to drive him to you. With your fenced-in yard, you have the best chance of capturing him. Would you be okay with this plan?"

"I'm willing to try. But, what should I do if I capture him?"

"Call me or Stan. We'll come right away. There's a gal in town who has always raised beagles. She may be willing to adopt him."

"Let's do it!" Carey smiled encouragingly at Marcia, crouched on the ground, petting the pup lying on her side, obviously enjoying the attention.

Stan gave his leash a light tug and the fluffy, thick-coated, black and white dog leapt to her feet. Stan turned slightly to look at Carey. "Just be patient. He has to learn to trust you. It takes time. If he's close by, give me a call. Maybe we can corral him working together."

"I will, Stan. Thanks! I've never caught a stray dog before. To be honest, I'm probably as afraid of him as he is of me."

"Call Stan. He is an excellent dog catcher." As Marcia stood up, the yellow mixed lab instantly jumped to her feet, tail wagging, sweeping back and forth in broad strokes above her hindquarters. The two waved goodbye and walked eastbound toward the ocean to take their dogs for a run on the beach.

Later that afternoon when Carey stepped out onto her porch to check for the beagle, she could hear distant laughter coming from the shoreline. It was much quieter now compared to the summer months when noisy tourists descended upon Ocean Dunes to relish in the warmth of the sun, take a dip in the ocean, and listen to the sound of the pounding surf interrupted by the occasional shrill chirp of the lifeguard whistles. Carey favored the off-season spending time with close friends, reclining on a wooly blanket on the beach, feeling the cool sand against her warm skin and watching the occasional frolicking of dogs in the surf. If she could only capture the stray this winter, it would be the perfect way to end the season.

A neighbor phoned Carey to report a beagle sighting in the little park down the street. Carey immediately called Stan, who agreed to meet her there. She grabbed a leash, squeaky toy, dog treats, and her cell phone as she ran out the door and down the street toward the park.

A minor storm had blown through town the previous night. The park grounds were covered in a light, white powder. Tips of green grass were still visible on the slopes leading into the area.

Carey spotted Stan, leash in hand, on the other side of the park and quickly walked over to him. "Do you see him?"

"Nope. Not hide nor hair." Stan scanned the area in a slow, panoramic motion. His eyes searched for any sign of the lost animal.

The stray beagle had been roaming the streets of Ocean Dunes for over two months. He wore a dark, tattered, canvas collar with what appeared to be a dog tag hanging down. He had tan, black and white patterned fur and large, droopy ears typical of the breed. He appeared to be older, but remained muscular, energetic and agile. He was frequently seen wandering around town, often circling the little, spring-fed lake.

Carey began walking in larger and larger loops around the park's playground, frantically squeaking the dog toy.

"Carey! Over here!" Stan pointed to the ground. "Look at this." He bent down and gazed at a line of fresh paw prints in the snow, gently touching the varied, round indentations with his right index finger. "He's definitely been here. And he's been walking in bigger and bigger circles. The prints disappear onto the pavement."

"We just missed him! That's so disappointing!"

Stan stood up and patted Carey's shoulder. "We'll have another chance."

After the other neighbors stopped feeding him, Carey could count on the beagle visiting her house every morning, assuming he'd survived the prior winter's night. She'd been feeding and trying to capture him since November. Three months later, Humphrey (the name her son had bestowed upon the stray) continued to visit daily. He had survived violent snow storms; chilling, whipping, fifty mile-per-hour winds; and consecutive days of below-freezing temperatures. His once-bright, cheery eyes looked sunken in and his plump cheeks sagged. Grey splotches appeared on the fur of his once all-tan muzzle. His bony ribs protruded through his dull coat. Carey noticed that Humphrey moved more slowly and had developed a slight limp. The life of a stray was taking its toll. When Carey retrieved the dog food bowl one night, she found a puddle of bright, red blood pooling in the bottom. Assuming that the dry dog food had made his mouth bleed, she began feeding him wet food. She worried that he might be injured or ill.

Carey was absolutely determined to capture Humphrey. She had learned a lot about him over the past three months. He preferred beef over chicken, Royal Blue and Taste of the West over other brands. He also loved peanut butter. She often left peanut butter treats beside Humphrey's bowl, which he always carried away, tail wagging gleefully as he trotted down the street. The front of the peanut butter treat box included a photo of a beagle. Carey viewed this as a good omen. She *was* going to catch Humphrey.

In the early evening hours as darkness descended, fewer people ventured out onto the beach to chat with friends or play fetch with their dogs. Those who did always stopped by Carey's yard for an update on the stray. She explained how she had been able to lure the dog four feet into her yard by moving the bowl a few inches away from the gate each day. She described how she carefully placed food and water on her lawn with the gate tied open wide enough for the dog to slip inside. Mostly, Carey shared the frustration she felt from multiple, unsuccessful attempts to capture Humphrey. Every time she opened the front door or appeared around the side of the house, the stray beagle always panicked and fled.

In late February Carey spoke with Tom, her youngest son, who had left the beach to start his sophomore year in college. He was a devout animal lover, often watching episodes of *The Dog Whisperer* and fancying himself as an "up and coming, new age, Cesar Millan." Carey knew that her son was empathetic and would understand her exasperation in being unable to capture Humphrey.

"I've tried and tried. I just can't get close enough to him! When I open the front door, he runs away. I can't get to the gate fast enough to close it!" Carey spoke rapidly. She was discouraged by so many failed rescue efforts while Humphrey's health deteriorated in front of her eyes.

"Mom, I'm coming down this weekend. I'll help you. We'll get him. I promise. Humphrey will have a new home next week. He'll be inside where it's warm. He'll be loved like he was before."

Carey smiled, as tears welled up in her eyes. "See you Friday. I love you."

"I love you too, Mom."

A few days later, Tom and his girlfriend, Kat, arrived as promised. Tom was tall, muscular, and athletic. He had light-brown hair, green eyes, a handsome face, and masculine jaw. Friends typically described him as warm, friendly, and charismatic. On Saturday, February 27, Tom prepared for the capture. Since Humphrey always showed up around 9:00 AM, he started getting ready an hour earlier. He parked his mom's jeep on the driveway, carefully positioning it at an angle so he could easily view the gate opening. He tied a string to the gate, wrapping it around a few wood slats, then pulled the string tight through a small crack at the top of the driver's-side window. The taut string kept the gate wide open. He placed the dog food just far enough inside so the door wouldn't hit Humphrey's backside when it shut.

He instructed Kat and his mom to assume look-out positions from the second floor windows and advise him regarding Humphrey's arrival and movements via text messages. "When I get him in the yard, I want you both to stay in the house. It's important that he gets comfortable with me first."

"What if he becomes aggressive and tries to bite you?" Carey looked worriedly at her son.

"I'm as good as Cesar Millan. I've seen all the shows. Then mimicking the TV star's accent, he added, "I will put him in a calm and submissive state."

At 8:45 AM, Tom climbed into the jeep driver seat, adjusting it to accommodate his long legs and positioning it for a lengthy stay. He placed his cell phone on the dashboard for beagle updates. Then he waited, though not for long.

Within minutes, text messages appeared on his phone screen:

Today 9:10 AM
    Beagle walkin up the street – on your left.

Today 9:30 AM
    Beside the gate – don't move!

Today 9:33 AM
    B coming in!

As Humphrey began eating, Tom slowly released the string. The gate closed very slowly and quietly behind the stray beagle. Kat and Carey watched anxiously from their look out positons in the house.

The gate closed. Then latched. Humphrey was trapped.

The dog was so engrossed in eating that he didn't realize the gate had shut until he turned around to leave. He panicked, running back and forth and zigzagging across the yard. He repeatedly leapt up in corners attempting to scale the fence, but it was too high for him to jump over. The beagle was obviously very frightened. He began crisscrossing the lawn with increasing anxiety.

Tom calmly exited the jeep, quickly opened the gate, and slowly entered the yard. He closed the gate, testing the latch to make sure it was locked in place. Tom stood calmly in the middle of the front yard. Whenever Humphrey approached him, he gently extended his hand. The beagle started to shiver as the wind began billowing cold gusts over the next hour. The animal was walking in smaller circles in the enclosed space, eventually moving close enough to Tom so that he could reach out and softly touch his head as he passed. Humphrey paused allowing him to briefly pat him and then pet him. Finally, the beagle stopped moving and sat down right in front of him.

As Tom petted Humphrey, he spoke soothingly and reassuringly to him. "You're going to be okay, little buddy. You're safe from harm. No one will hurt you. You'll never be cold, hungry, scared, or lonely again."

He waved to his mom and Kat, still peering from the second floor window, and motioned for them to join him. When they approached, the beagle immediately walked over to them. Humphrey sat down and leaned up against Carey's legs as if to say "thank you."

Carey phoned Stan who arrived within minutes with Marcia and two other friends, Rob and Allie. They all bent over the fence to gaze at Humphrey. When he saw them, the beagle jumped up against the fence and pushed his head into their open hands. They talked quietly amongst themselves so that Carey could only catch a phrase here and there.

"Looks pretty good."

"Neutered."

"I'm guessing six years old."

"Nice disposition."

Allie looked up and announced, "I'm going to adopt him!"

Rob continued to pet the dog's head. "I'll take him to the SPCA vet this afternoon. He'll examine him. They may need to keep him overnight depending on his condition. I'm on their board so I'm sure they'll do it as a favor for me."

Humphrey was delighted to be receiving so much attention. He repeatedly rubbed his head into their welcoming hands. Finally exhausted, he pushed away from the fence, walked over to Tom and curled into a ball by his left leg. He laid his head across Tom's unlaced kicks and fell fast asleep. Tom knelt down, making sure to keep his feet still, and gently stroked the top of Humphrey's head.

The stray beagle's old collar, now very loose, held a dangling clip that had been torn from its leash. It hung several inches below his scrawny neck. Carey carefully removed and replaced it with a new one, gently buckling it around his slender neck. A borrowed crate was packed with dog food, peanut butter treats, warm towels, toys, and a leash. Tom guided Humphrey into the crate and helped Rob lift it into the back of his station wagon. Tom reached into the cage to pet the beagle one more time before Rob drove away. Carey noticed a tear rolling down his cheek.

The veterinarian determined the beagle had infected feet and a deep laceration on his gum. He also discovered that Humphrey had been microchipped. Humphrey's real name was Ted. Ted was eight years old and had lived in Ocean Dunes until his owners, Jane and Drew Mitchell, moved to a new house an hour north. On moving day, Drew had stopped briefly for gas in a town about 25 miles from Ocean Dunes. Ted had somehow managed to run away. The Mitchells searched exhaustively for Ted. But, it had never occurred to them that their pet beagle would travel 25 miles south, back to his old home town. After actively searching for three months, Jane and Drew had given up hope and assumed the worst.

They were ecstatic when they received the call alerting them that Ted was alive and well.

It was snowing again and beginning to accumulate. The SPCA's parking lot was now covered in a light, white powdery blanket. A black Dodge Durango slowly drove up the winding driveway through the wintry precipitation and pulled into a parking space. The path of the tires left an imprint in the white, fluffy coating. Jane and Drew Mitchell exited the car. The fortyish aged couple walked rapidly into the animal shelter where Ted's rescuers had gathered, waiting to meet them.

When Jane learned how Tom had finally captured Ted in the yard, she began weeping. She rushed over and tightly hugged him, burying her tear-stained face in his chest. Tom returned the hug. Carey could see him grinning over the top of her head. Drew strode across the room, patted Tom on the back and began rigorously shaking his hand.

Jane released her hold on Tom to turn around and face the group. "How did he ever survive?"

Carey explained that they had all coordinated their efforts to continually provide the beagle food and shelter. She described how they had worked diligently to capture Ted. She ended with her discovery that he loved peanut butter treats.

"Yes!" Jane said. "He has an absolute obsession with peanut butter. I can't believe you figured that out!" She ran her hand across both of her eyes, wiping away the tears to stop them from running down her face.

"I was planning on adopting him," Allie admitted. "I could tell he has a nice disposition."

"Oh, my goodness! So much kindness and love for animals. I can't believe all that you've done for Ted! How can we return the favor?" Jane tried to control her sobs as she spoke.

Rob piped up. "I have two suggestions."

"Whatever it is, consider it done. We want to repay you and thank you."

"I agree," Drew added.

"Why don't you make a donation to the SPCA for helping us with Ted?"

"Of course, and what else?" Drew asked, already reaching for his wallet.

"Pay it forward," Rob grinned at them then. His deep, dimples appearing on both sides of his tan, weathered face.

"You got it!" Jane replied enthusiastically, her eyes suddenly brighter.

A door on the far side of the room suddenly swung open and a shelter employee appeared with the bedraggled beagle on a leash. Ted went wild upon recognizing his owners. He raced across the lobby, dragging the SPCA handler with him. He jumped up onto each of them, licking their faces in sheer joy, going back and forth between them. The group watched the happy reunion. Now the rescue team had tears in their eyes and lumps beginning to swell in their throats.

Following heartfelt farewells, it was time to take Ted back home. Through the windows, the rescuers watched as Jane and Drew walked Ted slowly across the parking lot. They gently lifted him up and carefully placed him in the back seat, tucking warm, woolen blankets around his scrawny, malnourished body. Carey smiled when she saw Jane slip him a peanut butter treat just before shutting the door. The Durango backed out, the snow crunching under its weight as its crusty surface compressed. It slowly followed the winding driveway, turning left at the intersection before speeding out of sight.

The small team of animal rescuers emerged from the building together. Snowflakes swirled in the air. Sounds were muffled by the blanket of the new-fallen snow. Little, white powdery showers burst from the ground with each step. The group stood still and breathed in the cold, crisp air. The surface of the black asphalt was bright white. They noticed a narrow path comprised of little groups of small, round indentations embedded in the snow-covered blacktop, crossing the parking lot then ending abruptly. They each smiled, realizing it would be the last time they saw the stray beagle's paw prints in the snow.

RAIN WITH PIANO

Judith Speizer Crandell

ON A COLD, DAMP NIGHT, in December 1985, frozen rain coated the mountains of Colville, Washington. Five geese, three goats, and two mules sheltered behind a stone wall. Beyond them, inside a half-built structure, four people waited. Uneven, created by human hands, the wall kept in things like the designated inhabitants and their livestock, kept out things like the frozen night and uninvited guests.

A car's headlights tried to pick out an opening. Juliette Harris shivered instinctively. She wrapped her arms around her body as the car's driver, her new boyfriend Sam, found the rickety gate, unhinged it, and walked back to the car. Juliette's seven-year-old daughter, Michelle, sat silently in the back seat as Sam called, "We're here. Let's go in. It's freezing outside."

"Michelle, let's go in," Juliette repeated, when what she really wanted to say was, "Let's go home."

At 39, Sam, a part-time music teacher and a full-time insurance salesman, knew the people inside the wall. While he and his passengers slogged through unshoveled snow, he told Juliette, "Ruth is from back East, too. You have a lot in common. She's a teacher. And

John . . ." Sam paused. "Well, John gets lonely up here."

"What does he do?" Juliette asked.

"Takes care of the house, is building the house. They have two daughters. And then there are the animals. He's got plenty to do."

Juliette felt something protective, even defensive, in Sam's tone, but she didn't want to probe too deeply. She had just started dating Sam and liked him. Why not meet his friends who lived out in the mountains of Washington State, out with the great trees that fed the lumber industry? Why not let Michelle see there was a life different from living in a neat apartment in town with her mother? After all, they had come west for a change in their lives. Sure, Juliette said, they'd join Sam on the winding, dark climb up the mountain in his butterscotch Vega. And now, here they were walking up to the front door.

Sam, familiar with the house, the people, the animals, simply walked in announcing, "We're here." Juliette and her daughter followed.

"C'mon in, Sam," a gruff male voice answered.

Inside the living area, Juliette saw two small girls sitting on their mother's lap. All three were porcelain miniatures–white faces, black hair, thin bones. Ruth, the mother, had some gray streaks in her black hair and sat absently braiding five-year old Bonnie's tresses. The other daughter, three-year-old Katie, had thin curls that encircled her head. Juliette felt unnerved by this simple portrait of a wispy mother and her daughters and found herself hugging her sturdy red-headed, freckled Michelle to her side.

A well-muscled, square-jawed man with a black moustache and a green-and-black plaid flannel shirt sat by a baby grand piano that seemed out of place in the unfinished room with various-sized piles of lumber and wood stacked haphazardly in different corners. Cobwebs and dust and ashes from the wood-burning stove had settled everywhere. Gaps in the ceiling revealed pieces of a sleeping loft piled with old blankets and mattresses. A winding metal staircase led the way upstairs.

"Sit down somewhere," Ruth said, still seated herself, still letting her hands make and unmake a braid. *Energy,* Juliette thought, *lots of nervous energy in this small, wiry person. Why am I judging this woman, also a mother, a teacher with two waif children and a handsome husband? Why do I think something isn't right here?* Hugging her own warm daughter, Juliette moved aside a yellowed child's shirt and they sat on a three-legged couch propped up on the fourth side with books and magazines. No matter how she tried, Juliette couldn't shake off the feeling that the spirit of this place was permanently cold and dark.

Sam spoke quietly by the piano with John, who also hadn't moved and hunched in a corner of shadow. Juliette guessed John to be around Sam's age. Like her, Ruth was probably nine or ten years younger.

Ruth stood up and her two daughters rolled off her lap. *Very nervous energy,* Juliette thought. *We shouldn't have come.*

"Sorry this is such a mess. I wanted to clean when John said Sam was coming with a new friend. But I work all day around twenty miles from here and with the children, the animals, the damn ice and snow . . . excuse me a minute." Ruth turned around and Juliette saw a large gash in her pants, as if a knife had cut the thin material–something private and not to be looked at, but it was too late. Juliette had seen it and winced. Sam, dear sweet Sam, had told her these people were struggling, were good people with a hard life. Rustic, he said, back to the woods, clearing out the detritus of city life and over-crowding. Juliette couldn't breathe here. Nothing seemed cleaned out.

Ruth trudged up the spiral staircase and kept talking, the torrent unleashed but the words sucked in and lost in the rough walls as her husband and Sam continued a dull patter of men's sounds meant only for each other. Michelle burrowed under her mother's arm and began sucking her red pigtail the way she did when she was tired. *I shouldn't have brought her here. She's tired and cold and unhappy here–like me,* Juliette thought. But it had taken them an hour to make the ascent. It wouldn't look right to leave abruptly.

So Juliette stayed put while Ruth descended and moved quickly through her sentences. "When I was pregnant the last time, all I had were my size five pants, so I had to make do. Now most of 'em are worn out. Used to wear them unbuttoned. John told me how sloppy I looked. He was right. Big, swollen, and sloppy. Did you have a pleasant pregnancy?"

Ruth didn't wait for an answer. "Well, we were living in a tent, cooking food in the rain, in the sleet, in the snow. John and Bonnie were always cold. But John was never able to finish this place so we could live in it and wouldn't get wet. It leaks even now–you're lucky it's not raining or snowing tonight!" Then she said more softly, "He has headaches with the rain, just like the piano," she giggled. "I mean, rain is bad for the piano too. The damp."

Juliette noticed that the fingers of John's right hand were moving over the piano keys without touching them. She also noticed the piano was the only object in the room that was bright, polished, and cared for. As if connected to John, she started tapping her nails on a stump that served as an end table for the couch.

Meanwhile, Ruth continued to speak a cascade of never-ending words. "So when I was seven months pregnant, I went into labor and we had nothing. No job, no house, no money for the hospital. Just me and John and Bonnie living under an oilskin tent. A big iron pot to cook vegetables from the little garden. Awful! Thank God your friend, Sam, was around. He brought up a midwife from town and she delivered Katie right on the damned mattress. Not a pretty picture, but Katie's pretty isn't she? Do you want some tea?"

"Mommy, I want some food," Katie said. Juliette stared at the child's translucent skin, her small apparent bones.

Sam heard this thin plea and said, "I'll be right back." He returned from the car with a sack of groceries.

"Oh, you shouldn't have," Ruth said, somewhat embarrassed but hugging the bag like a third child to her small chest.

"Thanks, man," John said and with his blue eyes pulled Sam back to his corner of the room, back to the piano space. Had Sam told her any of the background of these people? Prepared her for the strange unhappiness that she felt she was drowning in? No. Juliette wondered why not.

Katie was seated at a table with berries and milk, and Ruth asked if anyone else wanted something from Sam's magic bag. Michelle was dozing or pretending to under her mother's arm and Juliette couldn't think of taking any of the food Sam had brought for these people. Ruth collapsed on her chair again, a balloon deflated. Silently, Bonnie crawled into her lap.

Juliette could hear John talking to Sam about the piano that was apparently broken.

"Oh, that piano. I think John married me for that piano. Well, my mother, having money and pianos over the years. I never played." Ruth's high-pitched laugh was unconvincing. There was truth in the statement and it hurt Juliette to hear it. At this point, Katie pushed

Bonnie off Ruth's lap and occupied it, victoriously alone. Ruth kept talking.

"I convinced my mother to send it from New York. The piano. She would be really upset if she knew it was broken now. I think it's just a key or pedal or something. Like I said, I don't play. John does. And we like the girls to hear music, to maybe learn to play. Just because we're out in the mountains doesn't mean they won't learn cultured things, you know?" So, Juliette thought, it was the piano, the music that Sam and John had in common, that bound them so tightly in that little arc of light reflecting off the beautiful dark instrument's surface. And Sam could perhaps fix it, make these isolated people's lives better.

Ruth placed a kettle of water on the wood-burning stove while John went to the kitchen. "John'll be right back. I'm sure he's gone to the small storage room off the kitchen where we used to live," Ruth commented.

Juliette gasped. "You lived in a storage room?"

"Well, sure," Ruth said and smiled. "It kept us out of the elements, you know." No, Juliette didn't know this or anything else Ruth was talking about and had endured.

John returned flourishing a mason jar with red liquid that he explained had lost first its clarity then even its translucence as it shaded through a cloud of dirty pink to a solid murkiness at the bottom of the bottle. "Made it myself. But as you can see, it's been around. Called 'mother' at the bottom. Think it's all right to drink?" he asked Sam. "Wait, I'll look it up in my wine book."

John walked to a makeshift compressed board and cement bookshelf that had a downward slope and pulled out *Pioneer Sprits 101: Home Winemaking*. He sat down with the heavy book. The littlest girl, Katie, crawled over to him and was pulling his leg but he didn't seem to notice. She laid down on the floor in front of him, curled up, and sucked her thumb.

"*Mother,*" he read, "a stringy, gummy, slimy substance formed by bacteria in vinegar or on the surface of fermenting liquids; dregs." Then he looked straight at Ruth and said, "Guess that's you, wifey dear," and handed Sam the book.

Sam swallowed hard and looked down at the wine guide through his gold wire-rimmed glasses and finally said, "We can taste it and see."

Juliette desperately wanted to grab Sam's arm and say, "Let's get out of here. I don't want to drown in these people's lives. Something's not healthy here." But she still held back, felt priggish and unfair. So when Sam looked her way, she smiled at him and tucked her feet under her and held her daughter tighter to her side.

"I agree," John said, "Not much harm in drinking the dregs. Always spit 'em out." He seemed more animated, yet only focused on Sam. No one else was in the room with him. He had moved back to his baby grand.

"I'll get some glasses," Ruth said. "We don't have much company besides Sam, and he's busy a lot." Then she added more quietly, "Really, if you weren't a friend of Sam's, you'd never get in that front gate." She rushed away to her kitchen cupboards.

Juliette felt the corky, murky mother touch her lips, but she made herself swallow. *It's unique and country-quaint to drink out of jelly jars,* she told herself. But she didn't believe it and wondered how clean the jar was.

"How about if I put on some Beethoven," Ruth offered, "or Tchaikovsky or someone? We've got a whole collection of good music. John loves his music. With the piano out of whack, well, we play a lot of records. I kind of like the sound of the animals myself, but it's good for the kids to be exposed. My mother plays the piano—right, I said that—has a new baby grand, so she sent me this one."

"Not even as good as the cheap booze we had in the war," Sam said to John, the words having a strange reverberation off the piano strings. Juliette had never heard about any war from Sam, but they had only been dating for a month. What else didn't she know? Maybe that was part of the discovery process, the eros of a new relationship. Now she knew there was a war, for Sam and for John. Did they serve together?

"Now this room isn't done," Ruth continued from some point in her loose conversation. "No. When I had a paycheck set aside last winter, I went to the city and bought this red linoleum tile to put down. What do you think?" She pulled out several boxes marked *Tile* from a heap Juliette could see when the blue curtains rimming the sink were pulled aside. Beneath it there were, it seemed, enough boxes to cover many floors in many houses.

"Are you sure that's not too much?" Juliette asked gently and was soon sorry she did.

John stepped away from the piano and said, "We barely have enough food and she buys a shitload of red tile!"

"If you would of left the house and come with me, you could of figured out how much we needed. If you'd ever leave the house . . ." Her voice trailed into a distant place outside their stone wall, into the mountains. Away.

"Let's not talk about that," he said gruffly and moved back to Sam, the piano, the sacred corner of men's space that held the two of them, the war, and the lovely music machine.

Dwarfed by the stacks of corrugated cartons, Ruth looked like a dirt-streaked little girl with tiny hands that kept going to her hair and curling the straight wisps that only straightened out once more. The tea kettle behind her kept emitting swirls of steam that Juliette imagined could twist this girl-woman into oblivion.

Ruth began again, "I'll just put these back," and with her feet and hands, she prodded and pushed her two heavy boxes under the sink, out of sight. No one helped her.

"We want to get tickets to the orchestra in Spokane and take the girls—well, *I'll* take them. It would be worth the trip for them to be exposed to good music. Poor Katie is so small because she was premature and it was raining icicles. But really, she is old enough to hear good music."

Juliette overheard staccato snatches of male sentences, short-hand compared to women's long-flowing dresses of words, she thought, the same vocabulary, yet another language.

Only quiet Bonnie of the three children was awake now, had been awake and silent, eyes wide and dark, sitting up straight as if she would never go to sleep, as if she was called forth to bear witness to some adult event that only she could make sense of.

"Why don't we take Katie and your daughter—"

"Michelle."

"Michelle, upstairs and lay them down on the bed together? Katie, the little one, won't sleep alone. She's always between John and me, but if Michelle's with her, she'll be all right. If John and I get up and leave the bed, Katie starts crying. Bonnie, she never sleeps, do you Bonnie-Elephant? That's our nickname for her. Does your daughter have a nickname?" She didn't pause for an answer. Meanwhile, her older girl seemed to be unreal, part of the chair. From that chair, Bonnie-Elephant glared at her mother.

Sam was summoned and helped take the girls up the spiral stair-case. Juliette panicked as she saw her daughter disappear into the gaping hole that was the loft. But she remained seated, not wanting to seem foolish, not wanting to insult Sam's friends. Meanwhile, she looked out a window. Was it raining? Snowing? Would they be trapped here?

Sam came over to her and sat down. Things felt better having his body next to hers–familiar, warm. She let herself be comforted by the contact.

John sat on the piano bench and had to face Juliette for the first time because Sam was there next to her. But he shifted his focus to Sam when he said, "Yeah, I heard the vets collected money for this granite wall of names ages ago. What good is it with the war over years ago and no one saying thanks? Ruth thinks I won't leave here because of that, the no thanks, the no jobs, but you and I get it, Sam. It's not that." Juliette thought John's voice was the saddest voice she had ever heard. It was the voice of tears.

"I'm planning to go to DC and see it," Sam said.

"Why?" John asked.

"To read the names. Find out who's there–and not there. Maybe to heal." It sounded good and right for Juliette to hear Sam talk this way about the war, the war she never knew he was part of.

Even Ruth, coming down from tucking the girls in, kept silent after Sam's words. Then quickly, John asked, "More wine?" and there were strange vibrations echoing his voice as he sat by the piano.

"What is that sound?" Juliette asked Sam.

Sam loved to talk about instruments. He quickly smiled and said, "Well, if you listen carefully after John speaks, because he's so close to the piano, what you hear are the tones of his voice evoking sympathetic vibrations from it. If you press the damper pedal down so the strings vibrate freely, it'll also happen."

Then Sam went over to the piano, pressed down the pedal and told John to sing "ah."

Upstairs, Michelle or Katie cried out in her sleep. Neither mother knew whose child, but Ruth said, "That was probably Katie, but I'll go look if you want and if it's your daughter I'll let you know." Whichever child it was became quiet. Neither mother escaped up the metal steps. There was something in the room, with the almost dry kettle that Ruth finally moved off the fire, and the distilled sounds of voices echoing, that held them there.

Ruth sat on a three-legged stool and continued pushing her hands back and forth through her hair. She began to fill the silence once more. "And when Katie was born, my mother came. She rented a trailer and the little baby and I and my mother and Bonnie lived there while John, would, like, build this house. He insisted on living alone in the tent. Wouldn't even talk to mom. After she left, I had promised to ask for that piano and she sent it. Even though he ignored her the whole time she was here. She said she'd send it for the girls–but she knew he played.

"My mother and I . . . we couldn't talk, you know. There was no room, no privacy. She went back to New York and we hadn't talked." Ruth sighed and crossed and uncrossed her legs. Then she started chattering again. It reminded Juliette of a suspended phonograph needle put back down on the record, back in the day.

"I used to be married to a medical student. She liked that better, right? You know, she understood that better. But this," her words went into the room, her husband, her children, and finally the jumbled piles of stacked wood, "this she couldn't understand. And when John and I rented our other house, she hated that, criticized that. Before the children. But buying this land, she said, was even worse, 'A tent for you and two babies!' Then she rented the trailer and stayed for a few months."

"Yes," Juliette said. "Yes."

Sam was once more over at the piano, over by John, and they talked their quiet men's talk and Ruth kept up her palaver. "One night it was raining so hard and the babies were crying and I wanted her to just hold all three of us. But she wiped the trailer counter, put away the food, wrote to my father, and went to sleep. You know, I just stood there watching her sleep, my mother. And John, he kept just hammering at the house and rolling rocks for his wall–you saw it right? If he had his way there'd be no gate. But I've got to get out, work, bring home food. He wants us to be totally self-sufficient, reliant on the land, never have to leave, the kids, me, him. But that's not the real world is it?"

Juliette said nothing.

John's sounds about names no one would read on a memorial wall far way in DC hovered in this space. And they wove their way through cracks in his unfinished house, up the spiral of the staircase to the loft he, his wife, his daughters all slept in. Then they briefly touched the broken piano whose taut strings caught them once more and hummed their one-note reply and Juliette heard it, felt it. "Out, out, out" was the cry.

Finally she stood up. Finally she ran up the staircase, woke her daughter and, holding Michelle's hand, walked out into the damp icy rainy December night, just outside the gate she had to push hard to open. She surveyed the vast mountains that existed outside John's wall. Once hunkered down with her daughter in Sam's car, she could breathe again. But it was freezing. Why didn't she take the key?

Dozing off for a minute, she was startled by a male face barely distinguishable peering through the windshield. She sat up as the door opened. Thank God it was Sam.

"Where's your jacket?" she asked, as he slid next to her.

"Are you crazy, sitting out here in the ice cold car with your kid?"

He turned on the engine and the heater.

"Are we leaving?" she asked hopefully. "Can we take Ruth and the girls?"

He turned to her. "John. What about John?"

Michelle snuggled deeper into her mother's side and sighed in her sleep.

"'What about *John*?'" Juliette asked. "He's crazy, and he's going to continue to harm his family, let them die even!"

Sleet suddenly began pounding the windshield, so Sam switched on the defroster. Then looking hard into Juliette's eyes he said, "If we take Ruth and the girls, then we've killed him. I can't do that to a brother soldier."

Juliette sat up straighter, pushed her hair off her face. "Then come back and save him, but we can't let Ruth and her kids be collateral damage from his war."

"Our war," he corrected her.

"Please, Sam. We can't save them all."

He pounded the steering wheel, then put his head down and cried.

ELIZA'S CHRISTMAS

David W. Dutton

IT SNOWED THAT CHRISTMAS EVE. On Christmas morning, I stared out our front window at the blanket of snow. I worried that my father would not be able to get home.

My father was a marine engineer working on the pilot boat, *Philadelphia*, out of Lewes, Delaware. He worked a two-week on, one-week off schedule. Rarely did Christmas day fall during the off-week. This year was no different. However, as in years past, he was able to get shore leave for the morning of Christmas day. Now, an unexpected snow threatened that. Christmas without him would be no Christmas at all.

I sighed and rested my chin on the back of the sofa. The country road in front of our house had not been plowed, but there were a few tire tracks to show where some adventurous souls had braved the weather. If they could do it, maybe my father could.

Our little farm was only about twenty miles from the seaport of Lewes. I kept my eyes riveted on the spot where the road disappeared behind a stand of trees. If he came, that was the route he would take.

I sighed. "Mom . . . he's not coming."

My mother appeared in the kitchen doorway. "Of course he's coming. The snow's just making it take a little longer. Be patient." At twelve, patience was not one of my virtues.

Minutes passed. I began to lose hope. Christmas carols played on the stereo while my mother busied herself in the kitchen. She wasn't giving up hope.

She began preparing breakfast, confident that he would soon be home. A sudden movement caught my eye. From behind the stand of trees, the battered, green pickup appeared, a rooster's tail of snow springing up from its rear wheels.

"Mom! He's here!" I jumped from the sofa and ran into the kitchen.

My mother turned from her work and smiled. "Of course he is. I told you he'd be here."

He was home, and that was all that mattered. Christmas could continue as promised.

And continue it did. Dad pulled the old truck up to the back door as I ran out to meet him. He hugged me and ushered me back into the warm kitchen. He kissed and embraced my mother but did not remove his coat.

My mother tugged at the lapel of his work coat. "Aren't you planning on staying a while?"

My father laughed. "Got to go pick up Mom. She's probably having fits by now."

My mother smiled. "Well, she hasn't called. That's a good sign."

We all laughed at that. My grandmother, Eliza, would call at the drop of a hat.

For years, she had written a local social column and spent most days gathering "news" from practically everyone in town. She was relentless. To us, it was an annoyance, and we kept most of our goings and comings to ourselves for fear they would end up in her column.

Dad kissed my mother lightly on the cheek. "I'll be right back."

It was an annual tradition. Mom Mom would be collected and brought to our house for a big holiday breakfast. Once the table was cleared, we'd adjourn to the living room for coffee, hot chocolate, cinnamon buns, and presents. The tree, sparkling happily in the corner, was more than willing to give up the gaily wrapped packages it had been guarding beneath its branches.

We'd then pile into the car for the short drive back to Mom Mom's house. There, Christmas would begin again . . . this time in her living room.

Mom Mom lived in a modest, carpenter's Gothic house built for her by my grandfather in 1912. Now alone, she resided mostly on the first floor, restricting her movements to her study at the rear of the house. Her study was the center of activity. It contained her desk, several bookcases, a rocking chair, and a divan on which she slept. There she carried on the business of her daily life. She wrote her column in longhand using an old-fashioned dip pen. She met with trappers, examining and buying pelts. These would be sold to buyers from Philadelphia. Yes, as strange as it sounds, my grandmother was a fur trader. The front of the house was only for entertaining, and that is where we spent the remainder of Christmas morning.

The crowded living room had remained unchanged for as long as I could remember. The piano with its vase of cattails and its many family photographs dominated the interior wall. The pink cabbage roses still spilled across the sofa and two of the three armchairs. In front of the sofa, the Duncan Phyfe coffee table continued to support the etched crystal candy dish with its colorful, hard Christmas candies and the battered Whitman's Sampler box that protected the post cards and letters my father had sent her while in the Merchant Marines. The colors of the Kirman carpet seemed as vibrant as ever and looked unchanged except for a large moth hole that lay hidden beneath the library table.

The Christmas tree stood proudly in the corner displaying a vast array of vintage ornaments. Below it, my father's childhood stable with its two-dimensional wooden animals barely left room for presents.

My father sat in an arm chair next to the piano, my mother on the sofa. I was perched on the gold brocade ottoman in front of the library table.

"Mom," my father called out, smiling and shaking his head, "whatcha doin'?"

Mom Mom's voice carried clearly from the rear of the house. "Getting my letter opener."

The letter opener was essential for the unveiling of presents. Used correctly, it would allow one to open a present without damaging the wrapping paper. This, of course, would later be pressed and reused.

Mom Mom's entrance was heralded by the tinkle of china as the multitude of plates lining the plate rail responded to the vibrations of her footsteps as she crossed the dining room.

"Got it!" She hurried across the living room and sat cross-legged on the floor in front of the tree. It always surprised me, that at 77, she could still sit that way. But she did everything from crocheting rugs to playing Chinese checkers in that position. She was truly remarkable.

"The tree's beautiful, Mom Mom." It was . . . as always.

"Thank you, dear." She looked at me and smiled.

My father snorted. "Thought you were going to let us put it up for you this year."

My mother looked at my father and laughed. "You know that's never going to happen. She's afraid you two will break some of her ornaments."

Grandmother looked stern. "Oh, pshaw! It just looked so lonely there on the side porch . . ."

Dad laughed. "I hear you, Mom." It was the same every year. My father would buy her a tree and set it in a bucket of water on her side porch. Every year, he told her he and I would be by to put it up. With her heart condition, she had no business trying to do it herself. Needless to say, every year she beat us to the punch.

Mom Mom removed one of the presents from beneath the tree. "Now, I wonder what this could be." She shook the box tentatively. "Heavy."

My father laughed. My mother and I looked at one another and smiled. It was the same game year after year after year. As soon as Mom Mom received a Christmas present, she would carefully open it–using the letter opener, of course. Then she'd rewrap it and put it under the tree for Christmas morning. She denied ever doing so, of course, but we knew better. It was all part of the game.

Removing the lid, Mom Mom folded back the tissue paper and pulled forth a large bottle of bubble bath. "Now what in the dickens does a woman my age need with this?" She set the bottle down and picked up the card. She squinted at it and then handed it to my mother. "What does that say?"

"Merry Christmas from Laura and Ralston."

My father laughed. "Mom, you can set that on the corner of your tub. It'll look real nice there."

We all knew that would never happen. Within six months or so, the bottle would find itself ready to be given again as a present. Until then, she would keep the card with it to be sure that it did not find its way back to the original owner. My grandmother had had that happen, and once was enough. It wasn't that she didn't appreciate the gifts people gave her. It was simply that there was no need in harboring something she didn't need. Besides, it was a wonderful way to save money.

Mom Mom finally awarded the gift a "well, that's nice" and moved onto the next present. This one wasn't wrapped. It was simply a thin, red box with a green ribbon wrapped around it. Mom Mom smiled. "I know what this one is."

Dad laughed. "I bet you do."

She laid the top aside and withdrew a handful of brightly colored sheets of construction paper. "These are from the children in my Sunday school class." She handed several to each of us. "Aren't they wonderful?"

They were wonderful. Each piece was folded to form a Christmas card. On the face, each student had drawn a Christmas picture. On the inside, they had expressed their thanks and love. The cards were sweet, and I knew they meant more to her than any of the other gifts.

But the cards were also a bittersweet reminder of a dream that was never realized. As a child, my grandmother and her six siblings had attended a small, one-room school two miles from her parents' farm. Being the oldest of the girls, Eliza often found herself helping teach the younger students. She loved it and hoped one day to become a teacher.

She even began saving some money in hopes of attending college.

However, life intervened. One winter's night, Eliza was awakened by the smell of smoke. Her room was filled with it. There was no time to light a lamp. She could already hear the crackling of the flames and feel their heat. Once in the hallway, Eliza could see the flames as they shot up the wall and over the ceiling. Suddenly, she felt herself being lifted off her feet. It was her elder brother, Harvey. Eliza clung to him as he carried her down the burning staircase and out onto the snow-covered lawn. Beneath one of the big oak trees, Eliza's siblings crowded close to their father. In his arms, he cradled Sammy, the youngest of the children.

Still holding Harvey's hand, Eliza ran toward her family. As she drew nearer, she realized something was very wrong. Suddenly, she stopped and looked up at her brother. "Where's Mama? Where's Fanny?"

Harvey reached down and wrapped her in his arms.

The fire marked the end of Eliza's dream of becoming a teacher. At the age of thirteen, the household had become her responsibility. During the construction of their new home, the family moved into the tenant house. It was small, and they were crowded, but they were together. Eliza was responsible for meals, washing, mending, and cleaning, as well as raising the younger children. Of course, they all helped as much as they could, but the bulk of the duty was hers. My grandmother remained as the head of the household until the last of the children had grown up and married. By then, she was well on her way to becoming an old maid.

My grandfather changed all that. Twenty years her senior, he came suddenly into her life—a tall and blond sea captain who owned three sailing schooners. They courted and were soon married. He built her a house in town, and their life together began. Eliza knew she was not only marrying a sea captain but also his ships and the seas they sailed. My grandfather was gone for long periods of time. Most of his voyages involved carrying cargo from Milton to Philadelphia, but sometimes he ventured as far north as Boston. My grandmother was used to a big family, and she found that her new life was a lonely one. She was active with church and its various women's groups. She taught Sunday school. She visited her brothers and sisters as well as her friends, but she was still alone.

Whenever my grandfather was at sea, Mom Mom made a nightly ritual of lighting the red, satin glass oil lamp that graced the newel post of the stair. It was her beacon to guide him home. One night, as she was lighting the lamp, she made a decision—on his next voyage, she was going with him.

My grandfather was preparing to leave on a trip to Boston. His schooner, *Frederica*, was loaded with bricks from the Milton brickyard. His duffel was packed and rested against the wall of the foyer while he busied himself with final preparations.

Upstairs, Eliza set her valise on the bed and turned to the mirror to straighten her hat.

Today was the day.

"Eliza!" His voice floated up the rear stairway. "I'm getting ready to leave."

"I'll be right there." She grabbed her valise and walked down the long hallway to the top of the front stairs. My grandfather waited below.

She was halfway down the stairs when he turned to look at her. A puzzled look crossed his face. "Where are you going?"

My grandmother smiled. "With you, of course."

For a moment he was speechless. "With me?"

Eliza continued down the stairs. "I'm sick of being alone here in this house."

My grandfather was confounded. "Eliza, the sea is no place for a woman."

"So you say. Molly Vaughn sails with her husband all the time."

"That may be . . ."

"So I'm going with you." My grandmother was used to running a large household and was not accustomed to having her decisions questioned. As far as she was concerned, this situation was no different.

Recognizing defeat when he saw it, my grandfather sighed, grabbed his duffel, and opened the door for her.

It was a good day for sailing. Mom Mom enjoyed being on deck where the breeze was delightful. She knew she had made the right decision. This was the way to live.

The voyage was uneventful and smooth. Eliza enjoyed each day and looked forward to seeing Boston. On their last full day from port, the wind was brisk and the waves choppy.

After lunch, she sought out my grandfather. "I'm going to lay down and take a nap."

He nodded but seemed preoccupied. "Good idea, but don't undress. Just lay down in your clothes."

Thinking nothing of it, she followed his directive and was soon asleep in her cabin. It was the first great wave that threw her from her bunk and onto the floor.

At first, she was stunned. When she tried to stand, she found that she couldn't. The deck of the cabin kept changing angles. Slowly she guided herself across the tilting floor to the companionway. After being knocked off her feet several times, she finally reached the top of the ladder and opened the hatch door. As the force of the storm struck her, she heard her husband yell, "Man overboard!" Struggling to stand, Eliza eased herself out onto the deck. The waves were enormous as they broke over the bow and came crashing down upon the deck. Then she saw her captain as he fought to keep the bow of the ship pointing into the waves. When he saw her, he motioned her sternly to go below. Obediently, she made her way down the ladder to her cabin where she remained until the storm subsided.

That night, as she lay in her bunk, she heard him come down the companionway to their cabin. Slowly, he opened the door and entered.

"Eliza, are you alright?"

She looked at him and smiled weakly. "Yes, I'm okay. Did . . . did you save him?"

My grandfather sadly shook his head and sat on the edge of the bunk.

For a moment, she was silent. The torment that held him was written across his face. "I think I'll take the train home from Boston. This is no place for a woman."

He took her hand and held it. "I'm glad. The storm was bad enough, but knowing you were here made it all the worse. If we had lost the ship, I'd never been able to save both of us."

Thus ended my grandmother's life at sea. She returned home to her daily routine of friends, church, and family.

Their first child, a girl, was born soon after. Ora helped fill Eliza's days from dawn to dusk. Ora was a beautiful child who gave a whole new dimension to their lives. Eliza was happy. She had all she could possibly ever want . . . a husband, a child, and a home. For three years, Eliza devoted most of her time to Ora.

Then suddenly Ora died. No one knew why. My grandmother always suspected she had been dropped while in the care of a friend and neighbor, but there was no evidence of that. The "why" didn't matter to Eliza. Knowing the reason for Ora's death would not alleviate the pain she felt.

My grandmother's loss seemed more than she could bear, but she rearranged her life and faced the future hopefully. She became involved in several civic organizations. These, along with Sunday school, church choir, and her extended family, filled her days.

My father was born in 1920. His birth came as a joyful surprise to my grandparents. The void left by Ora was now partially filled, and my grandmother faced each new day with hope and happiness.

Life continued as it has a way of doing. The years slipped by. My grandfather's voyages were fewer now, and he spent more time at home with his family. One of his schooners went down in a storm off the coast of New Jersey. Another was hijacked and scuttled near the mouth of the Broadkill River. That left only the *Frederica*, which spent much of her time tied up at dock. In 1936, my grandfather died from a heart attack while hauling in a seine on Broadkill Beach. It was another loss my grandmother had to endure.

She was alone now, but she had her son, and it was for him that she must live. In spite of her heart condition, my grandmother worked tirelessly. Her church and civic duties never wavered. She developed the fur trading business that grew and prospered over the years. Mom Mom did her best to provide a stable and loving home for her and my father.

Even today, her life was full. Her doctors said she should begin to take life easy, but she was adamant. If she couldn't do what she wanted, then she might as well be dead. Unsuccessfully, my father had tried to get her to give up the fur business, but she would have none of it. As long as there was money in it, she would continue.

As busy as she was, she still had time for the neighborhood children. They would gather on her side porch listening to the stories she told. Mom Mom could hold their attention for hours. She still helped them build forts under her grape arbor. When she grew tired, she would sit on the edge of her fish pond cracking walnuts for the kids to enjoy.

Eliza was a staunch member of the Woman's Christian Temperance Union. We all inwardly smiled when her doctor prescribed a nightly glass of wine before bed. It would help her sleep. When that didn't work, she would read murder mysteries or play solitaire until she grew sleepy. Never was she idle. It simply wasn't in her nature. My grandmother had been busy all her life. She would be so until the day she died.

Mom Mom laid aside the last of packages and stretched. "Well, I think this has been the nicest Christmas ever." She said that every year, and perhaps she was right.

Dutton

We were all together. What more could we ask?

Seemingly without effort, my grandmother got to her feet. "Do any of you want fruitcake? Margaret Rogers baked it for me."

"Just a small piece." My mother rose from the sofa. "I'll help you."

"You sit right there. I know where everything is. It won't take a minute." She looked at me and my father. "How about you two?"

I grimaced. "Only a small piece." I hated fruitcake, but I didn't want to hurt Mom Mom's feelings.

My father looked at his watch. "I guess I have time before the last launch leaves."

For a moment, Mom Mom looked sad. "Do you have to go back today?"

"Yes, I've got the twelve to six watch. I could only get home for the morning, but I'll be home Wednesday for the rest of the week."

"Oh, good," Mom Mom beamed, "you'll be home for the rest of the holidays." Smiling brightly, she walked across the dining room to the back of the house. As she walked, I watched the prisms of the chandelier as they vibrated and collided with one another. My grandmother wasn't as steady on her feet as she once was, but she was truly remarkable for her age.

My attention shifted to the door that led to the foyer. The ruby lamp, my grandmother's beacon for my grandfather, still graced the newel post. The far wall displayed two portraits. The larger of the two was of my grandparents decked out in the best of their finery, my grandmother wearing a huge, flower-bedecked hat. The other was smaller, housed within a delicate oval frame. This portrait was of Ora, her hand on the back of a small, white dog and smiling at the camera. The photo was taken shortly before her death.

The tinkle of china and crystal announced Mom Mom's return. She carried a tray containing three saucers, each with a piece of fruitcake. "Here we go. I'm sure it's tasty. Margaret always was a good baker." She passed the cake to each of us.

"Aren't you going to have some, Mom Mom?"

"No. The consarned stuff won't let me. I just don't understand why it should serve me that way. Now, if I was an old woman, it'd be different."

She would never be old. I knew that for a fact. She was simply

130

too busy to have time for that. Her column, the fur business, crocheting, and the church filled almost every waking hour. To this list had now been added the senior citizens group, which met weekly.

Taking the last bite of my fruitcake slice, I set my plate aside and stretched.

My father looked at his watch again and got to his feet. "Well, I think we better get going." He began helping my mother into her coat.

Mom Mom sprang from her cross-legged pose in front of the tree. "Oh, don't go yet!"

"I've got to get back, Mom." My father leaned down and kissed her. "I'll see you on Wednesday."

My mother smiled. "Yes, we want you to come out for dinner Wednesday night."

Mom Mom clapped her hands together. "Oh, that would be nice."

Somewhat regretfully, she opened the door for us and kissed my mother and me goodbye. "Thanks for everything. It's been a wonderful Christmas."

She was right. It had been a wonderful Christmas. Fortunately for us, there would be many more to come before my father succumbed to cancer. Mom Mom would follow eighteen months later, dead from what can best be described as a broken heart.

Drowned by Wine

Kobé burgers' warmth
on a cold day in Lewes
drowned by Tinto Roble wine.

Winter Sea

Winter fuels big waves
Cresting high across the sea
Blowing foam to land

DRIVING HOME AFTER THE HOLIDAYS

Dianne Pearce

My eyes like driving
on lonely winter roads
where, encased in shale,
topped with the scrub-like growth of evergreen farms
and the tired slump of empty apple trees,
mutsu, fuji, gala,
the road drops out from under the wheels in an alarming way,
making my breath catch,
and when the car touches down again it's as if it is planing
skimming the road
here on watery, there on icy, glittering sheets.
When the car rises again
the red clay silos of Pennsylvania present themselves to me
a surprise bit of faded color among the five-o'clock-shadow
of the leftover stubs of crispy corn fields mowed late in fall.
As the car moves up and down
the washed out blue of the sky slips
between the soft swells of the worn-down mountains
brushing up against the ground.
My eyes roll along the road's swells and curves
like the carefully hoarded acorn
the white-eared squirrel by the side of the road
dropped from his mouth so he could
twitch his nose disapprovingly at the rush of cold air
made by my car slipping and sliding by.

Sometimes it is almost too much to see.
The sharp wind stings my eyes,
the landscape as bare, naked, and unbending
as being beneath a man
heartbeat tuned to the radial thump,
hair streaming down behind me like wind,
face pressed into the rhythmic road
of neck curving into broad shoulder.

DIGGIN' OUT THE DOG

Dianne Pearce

When the winter wind does blow
I throw the dog into the snow
The snow that is a'fallin' down
In drifts of 4 feet on the ground.

I let her out
But she won't go
And so I toss her
Into the snow.

Once out there she can't get in
Her little legs so small and thin
So in the snow that whirls like fog
I'll be a'diggin' out the dog.

When I finally get to her
She's frozen to the tips of her fur
If she was not ice-bound where she stands
She'd bite my pants' leg and my hands

As soon as she is back inside
She barks at me, then runs to hide
'cause when the winter wind does blow
I toss my dog into the snow.

AFTER YOU LEAVE THE WORLD

Dianne Pearce

Through the window I can see the bare tree limbs
Glowing white
Like splintered chicken bones
Cutting up the settling dusk
Their marrow seeping out into the cold
Bringing down the dark
It will be this way.
I know
It will always be this way
My breathing in
Like a harsh intake
Of something foreign and malicious
Sliver of white ice
Lodged there forever
Blocking the air.

WINTERS ATTIC
(Excerpts from forthcoming book)

D. Beals

SLICE BY SLICE

When young we are peeling our onion
Figuring out who we are
Layer by layer

We may get down to the center of the onion
Or we may not
But it appears worth the effort

But if life catches us faster than our knife
We are at a standstill
Life stops

Then life starts again now taking a bit of us
One slice at a time
One bit of our onion at a time

And the identity we worked so hard to figure out
Becomes the past
We become someone else

We begin to work on retaining the present
Keeping ourselves cool and a bit in the dark
Keeping as much of who we are

Even when it's hard
Harder than anything we have done before
We hold onto what we have as best we can

Though we know it's just a matter of time
Before the next slice is taken

MAGNOLIA TREE

Just look at them, the broken magnolia branches still in full bloom
Who tore them down?
She was upset, that was clear
That tree represented big parts of their history, they were siblings
The tree was a place of celebration, their 10th birthday party under its enormous fragrant branches
She remembered the time they drew alphabet letters on its fallen leaves
The winter their dad died, beads of sweat falling from her brow
She didn't know what would happen next
Who tore down those beautiful magnolia branches?
Fear swelled and drops fell to the ground

STIRRINGS

It is the year that I awake at 4:46 am most mornings; a time I have
never known before
The year that change stirred in the background and stirred until my
body shook with its power
The year that distance became a metaphor for life and death

It was the year that I sighed and kept on sighing until there was no
breath left to exhale
It is the year that past tense became present tense, and became past
tense again
It is the year that things really became 'things' and no more

It is the year that I was and am forced to face the needs of others
with little regard to my own feelings, no matter how I am treated
It is the year that tolerance for gossip, sarcasm, and idle chatter have
become too hard to bare
It is the year that I question everything, yes, again everything, and
everything again

It is the year that will make me what I will become
It is the year that will start a new chapter, the story unknown

THE CHRISTMAS LETTER I NEVER SENT

Carrie Sz Keane

Dearest loved ones, kindred friends, sanguine spirits:

I'm sorry I haven't been in touch. Time and the days get away from us. Now, here it is, Christmas again, winter, cold, daylight scarce, and I sit to type an account of our past year.

JANUARY
IVF attempted. Two embryos implanted.

I dreamed of what we'd name the children. If they were twins, perhaps Thomas and Phyllis, after Jimmy's dad and my mom. I have always liked the name Fern, but Fern Keane sounds like a bad verb when you say it aloud. Arbor is also quite nice, unusual, meaningful. Latin for tree, a garden arch.

FEBRUARY
IVF failed.
The pregnancy test was negative on Valentine's Day. I was alone, driving on the turnpike when the clinic calls to tell me. I stifled the crying. I never thought it would actually work anyway, having always

believed in nature over science. It was a fifteen-thousand-dollar shot in the dark. A colossal waste, in retrospect.

We became great aunt and great uncle to baby Ryleigh.

I stood as godmother to baby Thomas Leo, my best friend's second son. He was named after his father, Tom, who was dying of peritoneal cancer. In church we stood in a line for photos and we prayed, knowing full well that the prayers would not work.

MARCH

I flew to Toledo for the Hope Springs Goddess Retreat in Central Ohio with my other best friend, Kelly, from high school. We blissed out in ritualistic women circles, candle burnings, healing touch, Goddess worship, organics, labyrinths, a hot tub under the stars, gemstone divination, and ceremony. The time with my dear friend, in a gem of a hippy enclave, in the woods, healed me right up. No cell phone or internet for four days. We stayed up all night under a full moon and talked and drank wine, and sang songs. I drew the card Eostre, who happens to be the Goddess of Spring and Fertility. She surrounds herself with animals and gardens, collecting flowers and sprinkling seeds. The card said, "It is the perfect time for you to start new projects, access new ideas, and give birth to new conditions."

This month began a big push in Delaware to "legalize" home birth midwifery. I spent a lot of evenings in attendance at meetings with the state legislature, at Delaware State University, and in people's homes.

APRIL

I took a weekend trip to Detroit to visit a friend. It was spring . . . the city trying to spring back to life. It happened to be the time of year for rebirth and the sprouting of new growth from the decay of winter. I was astounded at the collapse of beautiful architecture, the demise of wealth and vibrance, but I was inspired by the spirit of renewal, by the growth coming up through the cracks in the cement. I visited the boy I used to babysit, Brandon, who is now working as an ER doctor in inner city Detroit, specializing in knife wounds and especially eviscerations. We shared "war" stories of working the front lines of healthcare and bonded over the drudgery of our calling. We talked about our hope to do third-world health work one day. After a few beers and reminiscence, Brandon told me that he held me in high esteem and that he used me as a threshold with which to compare other women. I stayed with my friend, Angie, who opened up a delightful bakery and pop-up coffee shop in a poor neighborhood in the city, starting with some free art, and good heart, and very little money. I left Michigan inspired to "give birth to new conditions."

I returned to learn that my midwife work partner got fired for "complaining."

We took a road trip to Asheville, North Carolina, with Lauren and the nieces. What an amazing town, tucked into the valley of the Smokey Mountains. They have a vibrant art scene, beer scene, and music scene. I copied down the number of the local birth center, thinking I should send my resume when I got home. Jimmy and I both agreed that we could see ourselves living here. We went white water rafting for the first time in Pisgah National Forest and spent a good deal of a day in a fantastic bookstore called Malaprop. I bought some gemstones to add to my bag, including a shiva lingam stone which was supposed to increase my vitality and pranic energy. The time off, well deserved. Driving home, Google Maps failed us when we lost satellite Wi-Fi in the mountains. We got so tremendously lost in the Appalachians, stressing, considering we had a twelve-hour drive ahead of us and work in the morning. Serendipitously, at a gas stop in a town called Hot Springs, we encountered Appalachia Trail thru-hikers making their first town crossing. Jimmy had just made a joke, "We are getting ready to pass gas." We vowed to hike the AT together one day, with an atlas and no worthless cell phones. Our vitality awakened. We had a one-hour car conversation listing malapropisms, like to say "dance the flamingo" instead of dance the flamenco. My favorite, when I asked some dinner guests if they wanted more placenta instead of polenta. We recalled the time when we went to a whiskey bar in Pittsburgh that was serving wood-smoked bourbon specials. The bartender recited the options, "Applewood, cedar, pecan, or *mystique*." Jimmy told me about a John Prine song in which a woman mistook the lyrics, "a half an inch of water" as "a happy enchilada." Somehow, after driving for hours, laughing and talking through winding mountains, we ended up in Knoxville, Tennessee. We called out sick the next day. Or is it, we called *in* sick the next day?

MAY

The second weekend in May is always our Annual Girl's Mushroom Hunt in Canaan Valley, West Virginia. The previous month, while we were planning our trip, I sent a text to the others and my phone autocorrected it from, "Looking forward to going morel hunting" to "Looking forward to going motel hunting." We like to say that we hunt mushrooms because we don't have any morels. The mushrooms were elusive. They hid from us. We worked very hard with our heads looking at the ground, and hiked many miles along the river to find what cooked down to be only a handful of mushrooms in the pan. We made jokes about the mushrooms being aliens, that they don't really exist, that they live only in our imaginations, but just when we were about to give up on finding any, we found two more and we were driven to keep looking. Wading knee-deep across the river, still very cold from the mountain-snow run off, I saw a rainbow trout in a shallow eddy. I marveled at how the colors glistening on the sides of the fish are in fact of the rainbow. I made an attempt to bend down and catch it with my bare hands, but it swam away too fast. We foraged wild herbs, mullein leaves to stave off colds, violets for jelly-making. We used spoons to dig the tiny onion bulbs of ramps from a shady hillside.

Back in the cabin we set up *mise en place* to prepare our foraged meal. The French concept of *mise en place* is a philosophy and system for what chefs believe and do, even going so far as to call it an ethical code. In the kitchen, the phrase is used as a noun, the setup of the ingredients, a verb, the process of preparing, and a state of mind. The afternoon sun beamed through the back window and hit the pine kitchen table. I photographed Jenny sitting in the light, reading a map. With her chlorine-bleached blond hair, she looked like a ray of sunshine. "What is the only thing that can enter through a closed window without breaking it?" I ask. "A sunbeam," I answered myself. Kate stood at the sink, rinsing fiddlehead ferns.

Alas, we didn't do a good enough job washing out the silt from the morels before we made the most beautiful-looking wild mushroom and goat cheese frittata, with fresh chicken eggs from our backyard chickens. The whole thing was inedible and had to be thrown away. Lesson learned. The hunt and the hike are actually better than the product anyway. "The process not the product," blah blah blah.

When Jenny opened the woodstove to start a fire that night, she said, "Carrie, there's a bluebird in the wood stove." I ran to look. It was a purple martin, not a bluebird. But, I said, "I'll give it to you. It is a blue bird. I'm not sure why they call them purple martins when in fact they are blue." Jenny rolled her eyes at me and argued, "This is not the time to debate the species. The point is, there is a blue bird in the wood stove." She reached in and caught the bird gently between her hands, kissed it on the beak, and set it free. "*Vogelfrei,*" I said, a word in German that once meant free as a bird, unbound, but now means outlaw.

At the end of the month of May, I was driving to work on a rainy Friday afternoon, depressed about my bad luck at getting called in for a primigravida in labor at the start of my weekend shift. I stopped behind a school bus that was unloading kids at the motel where they live. The girl behind me did not stop, however, and hit me, going sixty mph, pushing me under the bus, completely totaling my station wagon, shoving me under my dashboard, and fucking up my knee. I watched the whole thing happen in my rear view mirror. I felt very little pain. It felt like it happened in slow motion and I wasn't in my body. Had the in vitro fertilization worked, it would have been an obstetric disaster, without a doubt. I would have been twenty-two weeks pregnant. I would have lost the fetus. I guess everything happens (or doesn't) for a reason. I called out of work and Jimmy and I went to Dogfish Head for a beer, because we could.

I stopped doing yoga for the rest of the year.

JUNE
I bought a new car.

I delivered my one-thousandth baby.

I quit my job.

I'd had enough of the patronizing and testosterone-driven comments. My midwife student, who was frankly pretty stupid, had been offered a job nearby, with a much better schedule and a helluva lot more money. Having just read the article, "Lean In," I requested a pay raise, and better hours, and was met with a condescending, "You know, we wish we could pay you more, but we can't." And, "You know, you're like a little sister to us." I told them, perhaps they could pay us more, rather what we deserved, or at least the going rate, if they didn't drive matching Mercedes SUVs or buy bed-and-breakfasts and candy shops and Louis Vuitton luggage for their wives. I think they got the idea when I moved to the practice across the street, making $11,000 more.

JULY

Brittanne's husband, Tom, died. I spent a hasty weekend in Pittsburgh helping her to pick up the pieces. He died just short of their third anniversary, leaving her with a two-year old and a nine-month old. The funeral felt like a screenplay. Tom had been married for thirty years before he met Brittanne. He had two adult children. And, as it turns out, a criminal history. His own parents, his brother, and barely any of his friends came to his funeral. Upon his death, we discover that Tom had a federal indictment from The National Securities and Exchange Commission for selling and losing over $400-and-something-million in fake stocks. Brittanne got exquisitely dressed in black for the funeral, and proceeded to get so drunk that I had to drive her home, tuck her into bed, and arrange care for the babies. She said terrible things to me, that the only thing I have to worry about is letting my cats in at night. I took a breath, told her I loved her, kissed her good night, spent $300 at the grocery buying her formula, diapers, and quick meals, packed her refrigerator full, and drove away, crying in my new Mini Cooper, all the way back to Delaware. I was overwhelmed at the adulthood of things, suddenly made real by the fact that my best friend is a widow with two boys (my godchildren), my hometown is no longer home now that my mom is dead, and I am living seven hours away, in Delaware of all places, struggling with my own personal turmoils, taking care of women whom I don't really care that much about, as they complain about not being able to eat sushi and their restless legs.

I was never so glad to get home to my chickens, my garden, my loving husband, and my silly little dogs and cats, anxiously waiting to be let inside.

AUGUST
Work, work, work. Sometimes, we went to the beach and swam in the ocean.

SEPTEMBER
We traveled to Ireland to see Jimmy's family and to attend his cousin's wedding at a castle in County Clare. We spent two weeks driving all over the country, visiting kitchen tables and aunties, drinking Barry's Irish tea, playing music, laughing. The night before we left, Jimmy's dad told him, "I am on the brink." This, of course, peppered our trip with consternation, and we wondered if my father-in-law would die while we were visiting his homeland. Sebastian, a twenty-two-year-old son of Jimmy's friend, came with us on the journey, having never been on an airplane before and wanting a personalized Irish experience. Ever heard the saying, "Three's a crowd?" Well, it is.

I got pneumonia.

OCTOBER
October 26 was the twenty-fifth anniversary of my dad's death. I was floored by the way time had passed. Twenty-five years ago, I was twelve. I placed a pumpkin and some chrysanthemums on his grave. It was the first time I had been to his gravesite in the past twenty-five years.

Jimmy's dad was accepted into a home hospice program. With the aid of daily nurses and visits from eucharistic ministers on Sunday, he remained stable, for now, albeit bedridden and empty of most faculties. This has been truly horrible for Jimmy to witness and to bear. It has taken agonizingly slow years to get to this point. He said to me, "At least you only lost your mother and father once. I lose a piece of my dad every day." He was right. Nothing is worse than dementia. If it comes down to that for me one day, please feed me some foxglove or put a poisonous dart frog in my palm.

NOVEMBER

I turned thirty-eight. This was a particularly symbolic year for me, as it was the age of my mother when I was born. On my birthday, I looked in the mirror and saw her, not myself. And, I realized it was because I never knew her before this age. We look exactly alike.

My sister, Lauren, finally received my grandmother Carrie's death certificate this month. I was named after her, although my mother never remembered her. My mom was only three when Carrie died. We learned that she died of "toxemia" due to "bowel adhesions" from a "ruptured ectopic pregnancy." She was twenty-seven years old. I spent most of my birth month thinking about my legacy, my ancestry, and my life before and ahead, at what is likely going to be my halfway point. I thought much about being childless, about my gene pool, and about who will take care of me when I die.

DECEMBER

It is December.

I spend this month gearing up for winter, hanging with the dogs, enjoying the wood stove, clinging to what little time I have off, eating. I make a lot of soups.

My new job sucks. I think I took for granted the "little sister" treatment I received at Bayside Health. The grass isn't always greener on the other side. Sometimes, as in this case, the grass is dead. I worked Thanksgiving and I'm scheduled for Christmas and New Year's Eve. I'm hoping for some kind of career miracle to land in my lap. Either that, or maybe I'll open up a flower shop or write that screenplay.

It is December.

This is when my amaryllis flower blooms. Phyllis Amaryllis, I call her. This is when the paper-whites on the mantle sprout and then quickly wilt. This is when the Christmas cactus opens its fancy fuchsia display. Hot pink, such an odd color for Christmas.

We don't decorate. Cutting a living tree and moving it indoors depresses the hell out of me, and a plastic tree is totally out of the question. We don't have children, but if we did, I wonder, would we play into the whole Santa Claus bullshit? Would we let them eat ham? Would we be the kind of parents who righteously ignored their pleas for iPhones and high tops? Would we buy them matching pajamas?

It is December.

I spend this month under blankets, thinking about the past year, and about what is yet to come in the next. I think about the real gifts of Christmas. About friendships and car rides and dinner table talk, teatime, and getting lost. About how the hunt is worth more than the prize. About God and the virgin birth, about Eostre and all the other goddesses, my prana, my love of my life, vitality, happiness, hippyness. I think of you all.

I probably won't send this letter.

I won't send this letter. Christmas letters are the quintessence of egotism.

But, to the ether, Merry Christmas and to all a really-truly, good night. And, a good year.

Peace,
Care

Icicle

The icicle drips
Clear, cold drops of water
Refreezes again

Out Out Damned Cold

We need to transfuse
our lives with heat-melting joy
to drive out the cold.

CONTRIBUTOR BIOS

BEALS

D. Beals was born in Brooklyn, New York. The daughter of an NYC taxi driver, she learned early that people can share intimate details of their lives in just ten minutes Hearing these stories started her interest in writing. To make a living she worked for local, state, and federal government, writing policy and developing new programs. She currently splits her time between Maryland and Delaware and is a member of the Milton Workshop and the Rehoboth Beach Writers Guild. Along with her dog Sam she enjoys a rainy day, good coffee, and a view of nature.

CRANDELL

William F. Crandell returned home from the Vietnam War with a taste for adventure, a skeptic's eye, and a hundred thousand stories. Completing a doctorate in history at Ohio State University, he was awarded a Maryland State Arts Council Individual Artist Award in 2004 for his mystery novel, *Let's Say Jack Kennedy Killed the Girl*. Bill has published numerous short stories, book reviews, and political analyses. He was awarded the PRIZM's Mark Twain Award for Humor/Social Commentary 2012 and resides in Milton with his wife, Judith.

DUTTON

David W. Dutton is a semi-retired residential designer who was born and raised in Milton, DE. He has written two novels, several short stories, and eleven plays. His musical comedy, *oh! Maggie*, in collaboration with Martin Dusbiber, was produced by the Possum Point Players and the Lake Forest Drama Club. He wrote two musical reviews for the Possum Point Players: *An Evening With Cole Porter*, in collaboration with Marcia Faulkner, and *With a Song in My Heart*. He also wrote the one-act play, *Why the Chicken Crossed the Road*, commissioned and produced by the Delmarva Chicken Festival. In 1997, he was awarded a fellowship as an established writer by the Delaware

Arts Council. In 1998, he received a first-place award for his creative nonfiction by the Delaware Literary Connection. His piece, "Who is Nahnu Dugeye?" was subsequently published in the literary anthology, Terrains. In conjunction with the Milton Workshop, he is completing his third novel, *One of the Madding Crowd*. David, his wife, Marilyn, and their Rottweiler, Molly, currently reside in Milton.

LEWES
T.J. Lewes attempted to write a biography while relaxing in a hot spring in Jigokudani Japan. Alas, the bio was stolen by a snow monkey during a blizzard. The author survived, the Bio didn't.

NORTHERN
After publishing the Executive Summary to "The Future of Independent Life Insurance Distribution," Bayne Northern transitioned from writing nonfiction to fiction. She is currently completing her first novel, *The Bitch Seat*, situated in the financial services industry. An avid short story author, Bayne is also an active volunteer of the Village Improvement Association, a resident of Rehoboth Beach, and a proud owner of Thatcher, the corgi.

PEARCE
Dianne Pearce founded The Milton Workshop. She is a graduate of both the West Chester University and Vermont College writing programs, earning an MA and an MFA. Dianne has taught writing in Delaware, California, Pennsylvania, and Maryland. She sometimes takes on editing projects for other writers, and has done both writing and advocacy for causes close to her heart, among them adoption, developmental disabilities, and animals. Dianne loves living in Milton, and claims to have read *Paradise Lost* in her youth, the real version where all the S-es look like Fs, which she says must count for something.

POLO
Mark Alan Polo has been an interior designer for over 30 years and is President and Owner of The Urban Dweller/Polo M.A. Inc., with offices in Northern New Jersey and a satellite office in Delaware. Mark became a permanent Delaware resident in 2014. A part-time writer for the past 15 years, Mark's recent short story, "Fifty-Five,"

appeared in the 2016 award-winning *Beach Nights* anthology (Cat and Mouse Press). His debut novel, *Mosquitos and Men*, is slated for publication in 2018. He is at work on a second novel.

SPEIZER CRANDELL

Judith Speizer Crandell is an award-winning writer and teacher of fiction, poetry, and nonfiction. She's received residencies at Yaddo, AROHO (A Room of One's Own), and a Maryland State Arts Council Individual Artist Fellowship for her novel, *The Resurrection of Hundreds Feldman*. She has performed readings at the New York State Writers Institute, the New York State Vietnam Veterans Memorial and the Washington, DC, and Cleveland Public Libraries. A journalist and Washington, DC, speechwriter for nearly 20 years, she moved to Milton, DE, in July to be near the ocean and write.

SZ KEANE

Carrie Sz Keane studied journalism and English at the University of Maryland and later apprenticed as a midwife in rural Kentucky before studying nurse-midwifery at Yale University. While at Yale, Keane was awarded a humanities honor in creative writing with her piece entitled "Modern Nurse Nancy," a story about working a night shift as a new nurse on a postpartum unit, which was later published in a Canadian nursing textbook. Upon graduating in 2004, Keane has been journaling and writing the stories of her work as a midwife and her relationship with her patients and the community of Sussex County Delaware. She is actively writing a journalistic memoir of her career. Ms. Keane works at Planned Parenthood of Delaware as a sexual health clinician providing contraception, annual examinations, STD screenings, and treatment for males and females.

YURKOVICH

Milton-based author David is the 2017 Delaware Division of the Arts fellow (emerging talent) in the category of literature. David began writing in 1992 with a focus on graphic novels and comics. His first self-published comic was funded by a grant by the Xeric Foundation in 1994. As a writer and illustrator, his works include *Death by Chocolate* and *Less Than Heroes* (both published by Top Shelf Productions) and *Altercations* (published by Sleeping Giant). In 2007 David wrote, designed, and published *Mantlo: A Life in Comics*, a benefit magazine to help aid in the medical expenses of Bill Mantlo (creator of Rocket Raccoon and other Marvel Comics properties). In 2016, David was among ten prose authors statewide selected to attend the Delaware Seashore Poetry & Prose Writers' Retreat. His short story, "The Last Day of Summer," appeared in the 2016 anthology *Beach Nights* (Cat and Mouse Press). He has published two prose novels, *Glass Onion* and *Banana Seat Summer*, with two manuscripts in development. In 2017 David provided an introduction to the second volume of the *Deadly Hands of Kung Fu Omnibus*, published by Marvel.

www.ingramcontent.com/pod-product-compliance
Lightning Source LLC
Chambersburg PA
CBHW070333130626
46556CB00007B/2837